Tales of
Urban Encounters

Gerry Marsh

First published in Great Britain in 2018 by Gerry Marsh

Copyright © Gerry Marsh publications

Cover by Artlings

ISBN 9781999623708 - PAPERBACK
ISBN 9781999623715 – E-BOOK

Dedication

I dedicate this book to Marcel Steiner. The only man to have crashed a theatre into a car, found a gig on a desert island and who ate a wasp with his ice-cream. He supported my writing by shouldering my metal filing cabinet up three flights of stairs.

A truly inspirational man. Thank you.

CONTENTS

There is a trespasser. I cup my hands over my

eyes and stare out of the patio doors. The garden is dark except for two spots of orange that betray the urban fox's position.

She sees me. Gives me the longest stare that makes the distance from her world into mine, before breaking contact. As my eyes adjust, I watch her slip across my lawn, run up the fence then hop onto the neighbour's shed roof. The glass is cold against my hands and my breath mists the surface, provides the vagrant with a Vaseline lens that lends a romantic air to her roving. Imagine being able to cross boundaries with impunity, plunge through the neighbours roses, rummage through their bins. Ignore the *Trespassers will be Prosecuted* sign and stare boldly into other lives. It's outrageous.

She drops down and disappears. I picture her trotting down the alleyway towards the supermarket. How she'd rise up on her haunches to stare through the glass doors and leave her paw prints there.

I have a hunger too. A desire to concoct fancies. I rest my head on the glass and follow her as she trails through my city, scratches for morsels of gossip and tugs loose juicy story scraps.

SUPERMARKET SPECIALS

It made sense to get the Valentine gifts from the supermarket. There were his points to consider for a start. Besides, Conn left work at 6pm, so if he stopped off anywhere else, they wouldn't be eating till 9pm. Too late. Anyway, he knew what he wanted to get Sally. He'd seen the roses delivered days before, that pleasingly deep, red colour, and they were doing *"A dozen long stemmed roses"* for £9.99. Pretty good. But probably best to start with the chocolates, the furthest aisle away, and work back to the checkout.

The chocolate aisle was packed with bloody people, all probably with the same idea. Now, what to get Sally. Not that she'd eat any of course. So he'd get something he liked. Good grief, a basic's range of chocolates. Only £1.99. But imagine. Imagine your partner came back bearing a box of basic range chocolates! Why did they even bother to stock them? Well, guess they needed to cater for everyone. Now... what to get. Conn's eye was caught by a heart-shaped box in deep pink and black with pretty scrolled

3

writing on it. Hmm, that looked good. *"A tempting selection of luxury dark chocolate."* Oh, they were plain, Conn didn't like plain chocolate. Still, perhaps... He felt the texture of the box under his thumb, a sort of flock effect. And it looked like the chocolates were heart-shaped inside. Yes, he'd get them, they said they were the *"finest quality"*, and maybe he would enjoy them this time. Looked expensive, but were £4.99, not too bad.

Conn had decided they were eating in. You just couldn't get a restaurant table for love nor money on Valentine's Day, and what was the point anyway. He much preferred a night in with Sally. And there was a special range of nicely packaged Valentine ready meals all sorted out for you, with a selection of fine wine ready picked. *"Create the Perfect Night"* range, it was called. It took the fuss out of the whole thing. Salmon he thought, he liked salmon. *"Luxury Salmon from the coasts of Scotland, enrobed in a rich white wine sauce."* And it came with a chardonnay. In they went, how easy was that. Two eat for £15. Nice.

The revolving DVD rack stood on his route to the Valentine card section. Conn hesitated. Yes. He could see them after the meal, on the sofa, watching something a bit romantic. But funny as well. He hated all those really intense, emotional movies, it made him feel all embarrassed. It'd make him sweat. He always sweated when he was nervous. That's why he was glad they had the 3 for 2 offer on *"Ice. Deodorant for Men. For the man who stays cool."* He'd buy them anyway, so the deal was good for him. Not that Sally minded if he sweated. Anyway, where was he? Oh, yes, something light. Ah, that looked funny, he could tell by the cover, *"Big Sue."* How easy was that. Hmm, mind you there was a special on *"Goodbye till Tomorrow."* Only £5. But maybe that meant it was no good. Sally would watch whatever he picked. No, he'd get *"Big Sue."* It had four stars and the review announced, *"I laughed out loud."* In it went then.

Conn weaved through the aisles back to cards, near the fruit and veg section of all places. He could see where the Valentine cards were from quite a distance, because of all the people that flocked around. He edged past the few pinky Mother's Day cards that were already in, and a bank of yellow that indicated the growing Easter section. Then spotted the swath of Valentine cards that were recognisable by their deep red envelopes spread out before him. Now what would Sally like? Something sweet, not too sexy. But he didn't like fluffy cards, no kittens or anything. And he didn't like anything too sentimental. Or big. Lord, there were some big ones. Crikey, that man was buying something the size of his shopping bag! Ridiculous. A medium one was the right one surely. *"To my True Love."* Conn felt uncomfortable and prickly. *"Love Always"*

"Forever" "Always Yours." No, not right, but what to get. He wiped sweat from his face, willing the right one to announce itself. Ahh, there. No message, just a thick, cushioned heart in red with a bow attached. He turned it over. Code T. What did that mean? Oh he didn't have the time to figure that one out. But he liked that the shades of red matched his main present to Sally. Now he had had to go to a proper store for that. He'd got her a basque in black and red. £39.99. No suspender belt with it, stay-ups apparently were easier. He worried about it. He imagined putting it on her, then felt all hot at the thought. It was too sexy for Sally. She was too sweet for all that stuff. Then he would dress her up in it, and then get angry with her, tell her it was too sexy, blame her, even perhaps... No, stop, don't think of that, not now. Just the thought turned him on, made him feel even hotter and more uncomfortable. Sally in that basque that was so wrong. She was a size eight. He bought all her clothes for her. He loved buying clothes for her, and he knew he should stop.

Right. The roses, then checkout, that should be easy. But as Conn turned, he could already see many of the big black flower pots were completely empty. Good grief, why hadn't he thought of that. Course everybody would be thinking the same thing. Oh hang on, it looked like there was one bunch left! Christ no, no, no. Greedy bastard, where did he come from! Just muscled in from nowhere and took the last bloody bunch. Oh yeah, that's right, pretend you don't see my dirty look, you big bully. Conn felt like punching something. Now what was he supposed to do. How

6

stupid was that. Didn't the supermarket realise how many people would be wanting red roses? And they hadn't put enough in. Why advertise something if you haven't got enough anyway, how stupid was that. And look, look at all those pink and yellow roses. Why did they bother to get so many of those, if they knew people would be wanting red ones? A dozen red ones. Conn roughly pulled a bunch of pink roses up in his fist. They wouldn't be the same and he knew it. No one got pink roses. Same price as well, £9.99. No, no, they wouldn't do.

Oh hang on, what were they? A knot of bodies were seething around the black flower buckets at the end of the aisle—the prime spot. Ahhh, more red roses. Conn pressed into the crowd, managing that modicum of etiquette whereby he touched nobody and caught no eye, yet got to the front. Oh lord, no, these were not the same. No, these were slightly bigger red roses. Good colour, all really uniform. He picked a bunch up and smelt them. No smell, but the petals were lush, plump and velvety, and the cellophane felt thicker in his hand. A ribbon garnished the bunch. *"A superior selection of long stemmed..."* Nice, very nice. But £19.99. Yes he'd get them. Time was getting on now and he needed to get back. Not that Sally would mind if he was late.

Conn went to the self-serve checkout. It was always less crowded and you didn't have to deal with people. He hated all that enforced chatty stuff you had to do as they swiped your goods through too quickly for you to pack things. Besides, he always felt like they were looking at him, and he didn't like that. There. Crikey, £59.98. Mind you, that meant more points.

Conn was eager to get home now and wanted to see Sally badly. He wasn't even sure he would have the patience to put the meal on, because he wanted to see Sally in that basque. The one that was so unsuitable for her. He wanted to feel its silk and lace texture under his hands. Sally still felt so exotic. She was just perfect. He wondered how long he would feel this way about her. Would it wear off? He took the short cut home, through the alleyway with the trash cans where the foxes hung out. He covered the quarter mile from the supermarket quickly and let himself into the hall of his block. Another 22 years and three months on the mortgage and his flat would be his. £182,700 was his last statement. £420 was the service charge. Still, the hall was still all pleasingly shiny and it was new build, so nothing to do inside. All very American as well, like the mailbox idea. Mr C. Sumer, Flat 22, his said, in small clear print. But he didn't want to check his mailbox now.

He lumbered up the stairs, hastily fumbling with the key in the lock. He could smell his own sweat. There was no time for a shower though. 8pm already. Now where was Sally? He'd found out about her online, and she looked perfect in the photo. He had worried about her not living up to her picture, but she had. Oh how nervous he'd been. That had been three months ago. Now, where was she? Ah there she was, on the sofa on the front room. Exactly where she'd been when he'd left for work. Looking good in her '60s baby doll style dress with pale yellow flowers. She was turned away from him, her jet black hair falling around her shoulders to the small of her back. He could just see a small pop socked foot encased in a low heeled, bar shoe, the sort he remembered his sister wearing for school. Lord, she looked good. So young and fresh, and... only £3,000. *"The perfect Japanese Love Doll."* 20% off all purchases if you buy before November 30th. Guaranteed international delivery. He'd got her from a reliable Tokyo company, with 97% satisfaction on the reviews.

Hmm, just a shame she hadn't come with any points.

A circle of rusty pelt. Two tufted ears. And one

orange eye plays lookout. She lies on top of my shed roof, the site of Smudge's former and now usurped dozing spot. I test the vixen out and soft step across the lawn. I am level with the Pyracanthus when she uncurls. Fixes me with that familiar unrushed stare and I prickle with unease. Perhaps this outsider studies me with too much consideration, perceives me all too well. A perfect observer. Well two can play at that game I think and savour our brief closeness that allows me to marvel at her sharp bristled red-headed beauty.

She's travelled a long way from the chicken house countryside to claim my city's boxed southern fried variety, I think. I test pinning ideas on her, because that's what I do. Make up stories. And distance allows you to imagine anything. This creature is a world-wide traveller, a desert-stalker, worshiped as a God here, persecuted there, The Fox and the Stork, Fantastic Mr and all of that.

She interrupts my imaginings, shivers her tail and sprays on the shed. I step back, irritated. Great, and what am I supposed to do with this wildness in my back garden? This creature that ignores any concept of ownership or simple boundaries for that matter.

I hiss at the vixen. She unfurls, then pours off the roof and down. No doubt towards the parade of shops where there's bins aplenty.

I marvel at that bold stare, the perfect witness to our parallel lives.

THE TRAVEL AGENCY

"Sorry I'm late, Miss Price. I walked into my bank on the corner with some cheques, only it had morphed into a gastropub. Then I looked everywhere for the post office, which was hiding in the stationers. You can't tell up from down these days, can you. Are you still free, or do you have another client?"

"It's no problem, Mr Peacelove, take a seat. Ah, over here?"

"Sorry. Blasted specs, can't see a thing when they mist up."

"Call me Fiona."

"Thank you, Miss—'Fiona'. Oh that's comfy. Million dollar question, Miss—Fiona. Very important for my wife and I, because we don't want to waste your time. So, if you couldn't find any Mediterranean cruises for under £4,000 on your er, Internet search yesterday, I honestly can't go higher."

"Absolutely, Mr Peacelove. Our motto here is 'Travel in Trust', our pricing is fair and simple, 100% guaranteed."

"Oh good. It's our 40th anniversary celebration you see, but my savings stretch only so far. My wife wanted to come with me today and ensure we got our Mediterranean cruise on budget, but her arthritis was playing up in the cold. Doesn't trust me to get it right, you see. She just wants to go somewhere to get her bones warm."

"Absolutely 100% no problem, Mr Peacelove. I am sure one of these suggestions will be your dream cruise."

"Marvellous."

"So let's run a few options past you first, yes? You are really going to love this one. It's the Majestic Imperial, which leaves Southampton on the 5th May and visits Gibraltar, Barcelona, Nice, Rome, Valencia and Seville, and Cadiz."

"What? Where?"

"Or, your other option, on the 2nd June, is aboard the Imperial, their 'Western Med' cruise, and visits Barcelona, Marseille, Nice, Florence, Rome, Naples, and Cadiz. Or, the Regal Queen, leaves Southampton on the 21st May, and visits—"

"What? Wait."

"—Barcelona, Venice, Dubrovnik, Malta, Rome, Florence, and yes, you've guessed it, Cadiz."

"I've misted up again. Sorry. What did you say?"

"Here, let me turn the screen around a bit more. Is that any better?"

"Oh, gosh, that's a lot of detail, I don't know. Are they all under £4,000?"

"Absolutely. They're all £3,999. Full board."

"So full board includes *everything*?"

"Absolutely."

"Good."

"Except soft and alcoholic drinks, and sweets and afternoon tea with the captain."

"So full board's not everything."

"Well, everything would be the All Inclusive Package."

"Which is everything?"

"Absolutely."

"Good."

"Except alcoholic drinks and afternoon tea with the captain."

"Oh. So, not everything."

"The top *everything package*, which has absolutely everything, would of course be the All Inclusive Plus Package."

"And that is—"

"Absolutely everything."

"What about afternoon tea with the captain? He's an elusive character this captain."

"100% guaranteed, the captain will make an appearance. For all those in outside cabins."

"Outside what?"

"Cabins. There are inside cabins and outside cabins. Outside cabins are obviously preferable because you get the view of the sea, whereas with inside cabins, there won't be any portholes."

"No portholes?"

"No."

"Oh, I think we might want a view. Her arthritis is so bad, if it's cold and she can't get about much, she'll want a view."

"And, of course, that means you get afternoon tea with the captain."

"Yes."

"Good. Marvellous. We are getting under steam now, aren't we."

"Sorry, just to let you know, I've only got till 1.30pm because of my parking."

"Didn't you park outside the shop?"

"Oh no, there's a double yellow line there."

"Oh, I wouldn't worry about that, I mean it's not a double red line is it? A double red line is absolutely really no parking, whereas a double yellow is more, well, probably best not to."

"In my day, a double yellow meant a double yellow."

"Yes, anyway, where were we? So, we've narrowed your choices down to: outside cabin and AI Plus Package. Now it's simply a case of determining your choice. There's option one: Majestic Imperial to Gibraltar, Barcelona, Nice, Rome, Valencia and Seville, and Cadiz. Or option two: Barcelona, Marseille, Nice, Florence, Rome, Naples, and Cadiz."

"Sorry? What?"

"Or the Regal Queen which visits Barcelona, Venice, Dubrovnik, Malta, Rome, Florence, and of course—"

"Cadiz?"

"You're learning Mr Peacelove, you're learning."

"And er, Fiona, will the weather be warm in May? What with her arthritis, we really don't want her getting cold."

"Absolutely. 100% guaranteed."

"Well, the first one sounds good."

"Absolutely. The Majestic Imperial with the extra excursion to Valencia."

"Extra excursion?"

"Yes. The stop at Valencia is deemed an extra excursion, so it's an extra."

"Is it covered by the All Inclusive Plus?"

"Sadly, I'm afraid the excursions are not covered, they're—extra."

"Maybe we'll pass on that? I mean she was very adamant we need to stay within budget."

"Yes but the ship stops there, so the extra can't be avoided if you pick that cruise."

"But if it stops there, doesn't that count as a *stop*, rather than an *extra*?"

"I don't make the rules Mr Peacelove, I only follow them. Are you alright there, Mr Peacelove?"

"Yes, yes, it's warm in here. My glasses keep misting up. Difficult to focus. I live in a constant fog sometimes. More and more with the passing days, things seem to become cloudier."

"Well, our job here is to make *absolutely everything* as clear and simple as day, Mr Peacelove. 'Discover with Confidence'—that's our motto."

"I thought it was—"

"—100% Guaranteed. So, did you bring your card with you, sir? Would you like me to go through the details and take a deposit?"

"Perhaps I should run this by her indoors first."

"I'm afraid we have limited time on these offers."

"Could you just run through it again, I—"

"Absolutely. Here's everything so far. So, the Majestic Imperial from Southampton on the 5th May. Will you be driving there, sir?"

"Yes."

"So, parking extra. Two persons. Outside cabin upgrade. All Inclusive Plus Package. Extra excursion. Will you be flying or taking the cruise back to Southampton?"

"Oh, I presumed it would drop us back off?"

"Absolutely. Cruise back to Southampton extra. Great. There. So the deposit for that today is a mere £500."

"Oh, that sounds reasonable. And the full price?"

"The core price, sir, is still £3,999."

"£3,999. Good."

"Except."

"Except?"

"You have to factor in your add-ons and extras and upgrades."

"So what's the full price?"

"Do you mean the *full price* or the *total*, Mr Peacelove?"

"What's the difference?"

"Well, there's the full price which is plus the extras and upgrades, then there's the total which also includes taxes. Are you alright there, Mr Peacelove, would you like a glass of water?"

"No, no, I'm fine, maybe I'm sweating a little too much and the heat is clouding the lenses. Makes everything obscure and impenetrable. Sometimes I find it a little difficult to make sense of things. There's a blur around the boundaries of things. A permanent corona."

"Absolutely. Great. Our motto here, Mr Peacelove, is 'We've Got It Covered.'".

"I thought—"

"So, here on the screen, you see the total. Do you see it? Here, let me wipe them for you. There. Is that better?"

"Dear God. £10,567! What happened? No—wait. Sorry. That's. That's not acceptable. I was. She was quite adamant it needs to be in budget, Miss Price."

"But you said you wanted, needed these things didn't you, Mr Peacelove?"

"Yes, but no, but—"

"This is the best core price on the high street, you won't find better. Are you alright? Would you like that glass of water now?"

"How much does a water cost?"

"That's funny, sir."

"She just wanted some warmth, a bit of Mediterranean sun. Under £4,000. I'm sorry, I am going to leave it—"

"Wait. There is a cruise."

"No, really."

"A real bargain."

21

"I'm not interested."

"Under budget."

"Core or total?"

"Total."

"Total?"

"I swear. Total."

"No more shilly-shallying, no more smoke screens, no more extras and add-ons and ruddy tea with the captain. Is this a travel agent's or a betting shop? I mean it, I am laying down my double red line—not a double yellow one, Miss Price. A double red line. My wife wants some sun."

"Absolutely. Everything. And sun. I promise. I have all the details here."

"My parking is running out. One minute over and those wardens are on you like hyenas. I can't see what a thing is anymore. Please give it to me straight and—clear."

"Absolutely. Our motto here is—"

"Does it have an outside cabin?"

"Absolutely."

"All Inclusive Plus?"

"Absolutely."

"Free car parking?"

"Absolutely."

"No extra excursions, but stops?"

"Absolutely."

"And back to the port of departure?"

"Absolutely."

"And the price of £3,999 is a total price, not a, a core one?"

"Absolutely."

"Marvellous. Then you have a deal."

"Can I take your card, sir?"

"Yes, yes, take the ruddy thing. I've been in here hours. I don't know up from down."

"I'll just process that for you, sir. Sit down, sir. Please. You don't look well. Carol? Carol, can you get Mr Peacelove a water please? Thank you. There. Better?"

"Yes, just do this."

"Absolutely. All done, sir. A total of £3,999 is the price promised, Mr Peacelove."

"£3,999."

"Absolutely. And please, take this as an *absolutely free* gift with your purchase."

"A rug?"

"Complimentary rug, sir. Absolutely. Confirmation and e-tickets for your Majestic Oil Rigs of the North Sea Cruise with Tug Boat Tilly Tours from Newcastle on 5th November has been sent to your email, sir."

"Majestic—Oil Rigs?!"

"I've been assured it's an absolute, definite possibility the arctic sun shines strong in November. Carol, would you like to show Mr Peacelove out please, he's having difficulty seeing things clearly today."

It is broad daylight, but the thief is bold. Is this my thief? I stand and watch as she lifts a pointed nose to the hospital bin and sniffs. She backs away and I wonder whether some acrid odour has proved unappealing. No, that's not right. I've been swopping fictions for facts because foxes don't do much bin-raiding so they say. She stops. Has she seen me? If so, she gives no sign and instead weaves that long, low body around a SUV then darts across the car park.

No meeting point today then. My feral nomad is too intent on tracking her path towards the next observation. It is a relief because I don't want that exacting gaze on me. Not when it's another bad day, a 'to-do list' day and won't bear up to scrutiny. A life whittled down to survival tasks is not as enjoyable as plunging into a world of stories and finding pleasure in fantasy. Is that the difference between survival and living? Does it feel like a life is rendered more meaningful or enjoyable when it's peppered with make-belief?

My fox is scavenging things, foraging for something tangible I tell myself. Yet still I imagine her prowling the streets silently attesting to the strangeness of our human existence.

OUTSIDE THE HOSPITAL

Holy apostle, Saint Jude, faithful friend of Jesus, the church honour and invoke thee, as the patron of— of things almost despaired of— Sorry, I can't remember the rest, my mother always said I made a terrible Catholic. Hello, St Jude? Are you there? Look, I'm most awfully sorry about this, and I know it's entirely my fault, only I think I need a bit of help. I'm hopeless, really I am. But as a Patron Saint of Hopelessness are you on 'call out' so to speak for hopeless people, or hopeless 'causes'? I'm not sure I'm a 'cause'? If you're not the relevant fellow, could you bump my request up to another saint? I don't want to bother the 'big guns' so to speak, I've got an awful lot of respect for Mary, but I'm sure she's greatly in demand.

Only I can feel my hands slipping on the drainpipe.

I'm outside the second floor of the maternity wing at Queen Mary's in Sidcup. Is it like Google? Will you need the postcode? I think it's the north wall because my fingers are bloody freezing. Sorry. Forgive my blasphemy. I don't know what I'm expecting. You'll arrive 'blue lighting it' from heaven. I haven't really done this very well, like maybe I should have tied a sheet or something to the hospital bed leg, like they do in films, not just climbed out, but, well they were those fitted ones.

Hello, are you there? If you're not, perhaps that could mean things aren't completely hopeless. Maybe I just need your advice? I'm sure you're a busy man and there are plenty of cases more deserving than mine. Sorry, I don't want to make a fuss and you'll want to know what's going on first, right, to assess the 'case'? Is that it? OK, I'll try and wedge myself better for a minute and get my breath back. I can put my toes in the brackets and hold close and see if that helps with the shaking. It's lucky there's not a lot of me, though my bump is getting in the way of gripping close to the pipe.

Do you think I should try and shin back up?

I never know the right thing to do in situations. I'm not sure I *can* get back up, and even if I did, I don't see how I'd get past my husband Derek and the midwife and the paediatrician, all waiting in the hall discussing me. I hate being the centre of attention. Maybe I'll just wait a minute, then try shinning down, yes? Is that what you think?

Sorry, you were assessing the case first, right, before attendance so to speak. I expect it's a bit like ringing NHS direct first before bothering the doctor. Okay, I'll start at the beginning, yes?

None of this was meant to happen you see, it's all my own fault. It had been a really hot August afternoon, seven months ago, and when I'd knocked off the production line, I'd been feeling queasy and out of sorts, because it always smells like dog food in Simmonds Factory, so I didn't head straight home, but went through Danson Park, then sat on a bench, and I don't know, just stayed there for a while, just daydreaming. I can't think what came over me.

So anyway, by the time I 'came to', the sun was hiding behind the climbing frame so I hurried home. I hadn't put Derek's tea on and he'd be wondering where I was. I'd got a bit of ham in the day previous you see. When I came in, I thought I'd got away with it, but he'd been waiting for me at the kitchen table, and stood up, with his hands on his hips, which always reminds me of a picture I'd seen of Henry VIII once, but anyway he's saying, 'Where've you been?' and on and on. I blushed, of course, because I hate the attention, which he used to like about me, my blushing. Anyway, I didn't know what to say, because it's appalling upsetting people, I hate upsetting anybody, so I just stammered out the first thing that came into my head and said I'd been to the doctors. I was going to follow up by saying it was about my bunion playing up again, but I didn't get that far, because I'm not good at lying, so I just stood there as quiet as a mouse. So he looks at me, and I know he knows I'm lying, and he says it. 'You're lying,' he says. I can't deny it, and nod and get ready, because I know I'm in for it. Only nothing happens. There's this pause as he's looking at me, and I'm looking at him.

Then his face lights up.

Really. I'd never seen that happen before to Derek, literally like some light in him had switched on, and he comes forward and he gives me this really big hug, and he says it's marvellous news, and he's been waiting, and he's so happy. Like deep down happy. You're 'lit up' so to speak too, aren't you, as a saint? You've got a flame over your head, right? Is it there permanently, or does it like flicker out when you need some sleep? Must be difficult to get some shut eye with a flame above your head, but then maybe you don't need to worry about those things. Maybe you don't sleep?

Hello? St Jude? I think I'm going to fidget around a little because my legs won't stop shaking, and wrap my arms round like this, if that's ok? Sorry, I've gone off track. Bloody simple my mum would say.

So anyway, I liked Derek's size. That's what I meant about being like Henry VIII, not like Henry VIII's height, which I don't think is true anyway, but his 'girth', that's the word. Girth. He's only five foot seven, but stocky, kind of 'meaty' and solid, and good because he stands in front and talks when we socialise, and you have no idea what a relief it is to have somebody talk for you, well, most of the time. Though I think I talk a lot in my head.

I think he liked my small size too.

Sorry, got to stop again, only I need to readjust myself. I can't see properly, sorry, I must look awful, tears are ugly. Oh my, oh no, my glasses have fallen off. It must be the sweat and tears have made my nose slippery. It's not a good look, and I want to wipe my face, but I'm scared to loosen my grip. They say never to look down, but I'm looking down now because there's bits of me that have left and gone ahead already. There's a brown blur which must be my left court shoe that came off when I first started down the drainpipe, and now my glasses have joined it. I'm glad things are blurred, because that makes this all feel a little bit less real.

Maybe that means you could turn up, and 'fit in' so to speak, with the—hopelessness of the situation. I'm bloody hopeless me. Sorry.

Lord, I really hope nobody walks by down there and looks up, because that would simply be the worst thing ever.

I keep looking up too, towards the window, because I don't know how long they'll leave me alone before they come in and insist on the examination. I said I didn't want a fuss and didn't want to be 'looked at', but the doctor just sort of laughed and said it was necessary to find out how dilated I was. I said I was Catholic, and backed into the corner with my coat still on, so then they became a bit concerned and after a while of conversation with the midwife and the doctor they called Derek out of the room, and that's when I saw my chance. I don't want a fuss you see.

Ah, ah, I'm slipping. *Pray for me, who am so miserable. Make use, I implore thee, of that particular privilege accorded to thee, and bring speedy—speedy help where help—* There. There's a ledge. Thank you.

31

I've got a cramp, but I think if I just let my hands and feet 'slide a bit' I might be able to get to the 1st floor windowsill. This bloody bump doesn't help either. Sorry. Was that the start of the 'help'? It's a tiny confessional-sized window, not one I could get through, but a better stopping place, and as I'm only five foot one, perhaps I could even squeeze into it for a bit. Oh, well, it's too small, so I'll just rest one 'sitting bone' on it. Sounds better than 'half a bottom, or one 'buttock', that sounds all wrong. Sorry, I shouldn't be saying these things to a saint.

I really wish I were smaller, or perhaps invisible, or in fact I wish I weren't here at all. Sorry, I know you're not supposed to say that sort of thing.

Does that count as hopelessness?

Maybe I need to be deserving. I don't think I'm deserving, although, ah, listen, St Jude, if I were to tell you that I'd made him a very happy man for the past seven months, would you take it into consideration? It was seven months of real happiness for the pair of us, which made me think perhaps he hadn't been happy for the previous eight years. He'd never said anything, but then neither had I. Him being happy made me happy, because I like to please people, you see, it's really not nice having any upset is it?

Do you have enough yet, St Jude, to make a decision? Am I worth a visit? Hello?

The bloody bump is pushing me out and over. I'm slipping. Ahhh, ahhh, *Come to mine assistance in* *this great need, that I may receive the consolation and succour of heaven in all my necessities, tribulations and sufferings—and—*Jesus God, I nearly, I nearly.

"Hello?"

"Hello?" There. A shape through the frosted window glass. "St Jude? Is that You?"

"Is there somebody there?" a voice says.

"Yes, it's me, Irene." Just in the nick of time.

"What the—are you on the ledge? I'll get help."

"I thought you were the help."

"This is a—I'm just—just wait," he says.

"Don't go. DON'T GO. I need you." I slap my hand to the cold glass.

"Okay, okay, don't—" he slaps his hand to the glass too, and St Jude has got long fingers, and a kind of thin pale palm. I'd have preferred a 'big boned' palm, so to speak, it makes you feel protected, but it's a miracle he's come at all so I'm not complaining. I can't see anything else except a light blue blur of clothing, so he's not wearing his saintly whites. Lord, the window is filthy, but I can't complain, the National Health Service do a champion job and I expect window cleaning up here is the last thing on their minds.

"You've got an accent St Jude. You must get around a lot, have you picked it up?" Because it sounds antipo – antipo – Australian. Shouldn't it be middle eastern or something? Maybe saints have got to move with the times, otherwise how would I understand Hebrew or whatnot. I'm surprised he didn't twitter me.

"I don't think I'm the right person for this, I don't usually—"

"Thank you for coming. I'm sure you know all the right things to say or do. Don't go. I'll tell you everything. Please intercede for me. I'm not sure I can hold on much longer."

"Hold on. Just hold on," Jude says.

"I need a miracle. I just want to know, Jude, can I pretend this didn't happen, and could things ever go back to normal? That's what I want to ask for."

"Ah, I'm not really an expert at these things. If you ask me, 'normal' can be a pretty fucked up place anyway."

This St Jude is quite blunt with his words, quite 'worldly' in his expressions you might say. So I say.

"I'm an evil, sinful woman, full of pretence." Simple too, and a terrible Catholic, according to my mum.

"That sounds interesting. How old are you?"

"Twenty-eight." What a strange question, but he's getting to know me.

"Oh that's a bit old."

"You'll be wanting to know what I've done Jude, yes?" I really don't want to tell him, it's so awful. But I need to get out of this—predicament.

"St Jude, could I start with a really small intercession and pray to you that nobody passes by down below, because if they look up, I've got an awful long ladder up my tights now, and I'm scared they'll see it, or worse, be able to see up my skirt, which would be mortifying and my old Mum would have properly shouted at me about that, if she'd been alive, which she's not."

"I wish I were there to see it," Jude says.

"What?"

"Nothing," he says.

I think he's joking with me, which is disconfab—disconfob—confusing, not what you'd expect.

"Where are you exactly?" he says.

"I'm on the ledge. The paintwork is all nice and cool on my ear, but my bump keeps getting in the way."

"Your bump?"

"Do you think I should let it go?"

"Christ, are you giving birth? No, no don't let go of anything. Wait."

"I'm sorry, I've got to—I can't hold on anymore, it's in the way you see."

And it is. I've got to let it go. It's me or the bump, because it keeps pushing me out from the ledge and I've got to grip properly, so I loosen my belt.

And I let it go.

It is such a relief to see the cushion go bouncing down, ricocheting off the wall. An easy birth. I can see it as a white blob nestling beside the brown blur of my shoe down below. Ah and the sensation of freedom from restriction is amazing, though my skirt is all loose and saggy.

"What's happening? I'm crap at this kind of thing, but I dunno, keep talking to me?"

"Thank you. I will confess the whole story. This morning I crept out to the bus station at 7am, everything could still have worked out okay. I could have taken the 26A into town, got off at the co-op and then crossed over the road to the National Express coach stop, and then down to Dover. I'd checked the timetable and everything, even got a ticket in advance. I mean I had to go, didn't I? There were only four weeks left before the 'birth'. Is there someone there with you St Jude?" I say this because I can hear a kind of gurgling from behind the frosted glass.

There are a lot of white shadows, so maybe it's a 'church space', because they have 'places of worship' these days in hospitals, don't they? Or maybe it's a broom cupboard. Lord above, what if it were the urinal. But saints don't use urinals do they? It's not nice to think of saints owning—parts, and I blush at my disgusting thoughts.

"What do you think will happen to the lovely brand new adjustable pram that Derek bought from the Glades?"

"Sorry?"

"Do you think he'll be able to take it back?"

"I wouldn't know."

"He'd bought a cot too that looked like a sleigh, and pretty, white bedding too from '*The White Company*' and baby-grows in the smallest size. All new. And he hadn't made a fuss, and I kept saying it wasn't necessary, but he insisted."

"It sounds like this 'Derek' cares very much about you. You have a lot to live for. That's what I'm supposed to say, isn't it? You have a lot to live for."

"He'll hate me forever now." Didn't Jude understand that if you didn't please people they let you go? Without Derek, I don't have anything to hold onto.

"It's not like you killed anybody, is it?" Jude says, but he's diverting me.

"But at least he'll get a refund, because I kept the receipts, and I left them this morning on the mantelpiece pinned down with the heavy donkey ornament, and OK, so some of the receipts are older than 28 days, but they should take pity on him, shouldn't they? St Jude, do you think they'll give refunds after 28 days?

"Yes."

"Can you intercede on Derek's behalf?"

"Yes, of course."

I'm thinking this is the most obliging saint ever, but concerned because this is a 'consumer' issue, and there might be a saint one is supposed to pray to on 'consumer issues', which is not a 'hopeless cause', and I'm worried I'll get St Jude into trouble because he'll be stepping on another saint's toes.

"If he can take it all back, well maybe one day he'd forgive me. I really don't want any fuss, you see." I stop. Because I know it's hopeless. Useless. He'll never forgive me. I don't know what to say and stop. Things hurt. The ledge. My head. My sitting bones. I just want everybody to be happy with me, is that too much to ask? If I could believe Derek could move on, get a new life—

"Does Derek like Sharon in Accounting, St Jude? Are you allowed to tell me that? Because if he did and he was able to move on, you know, after, well that would make me feel less hopeless about the situation."

"I don't know." I swear St Jude sounds irritated, and oh Lord, what if I manage to cheese him off too, he's my only hope.

"Sorry. Sorry. I'll carry on with the confession, then you can tell me what to do?"

"Yes, keep talking."

"Okay. So, anyway, I was going to creep out of his life this morning, only as I'm waiting there at the bus stop I see his Rover drive past, and he does a double take and screeches to a halt. I'm mortified, and hoped the other drivers wouldn't get irate with him because it was like an 'emergency stop' as my old driving instructor Les would have said. So he jumps out the car and asks me what I'm doing at the bus stop so early, and with a suitcase. I don't know what to say, so I ask why he's coming back home. He says he'd forgotten his gym gear, then stands there waiting for me to answer his question. My mouth's hanging open, I'm terrified, I didn't want any fuss. And there's these two women across the road staring at us, and I couldn't think what to say or do. But this look comes into his eyes, he does the 'lighting up' thing again, and starts dancing around, shouting, 'The baby's coming, the baby's coming.' Oh my, do those two across the road really stare at me then, and I find myself hugging my bump protectively, which is really silly, because I know it's only a pillow."

"Sorry? A what?"

"You know, a cushion." I can't help it, I start to cry again, because all those months carrying the cushion, well, I really did start getting excited too, and hoped and wished—

"A cushion?"

"So yes, he's jumping about saying—'It's early, it's early'—and I'm confused, I thought he meant the time of day, but he meant for the baby to come, and then he was saying what was I doing getting a bus, because he said he'd wanted to drive me to the hospital. Called me a silly sausage, but in a really nice way. Derek's been so different with me—from how he'd been before."

I hitch my shoulder up to try and wipe my eyes, because it's so embarrassing losing control like that. It kind of works a bit, because when I blink hard they've cleared, and as I look down, I see there's a man in green overalls below where I'm sitting on the ledge, and he's stopped. He's going bald on top. He's picking up the shoe, and he's looking up, and seen me. I really didn't want this to happen, I have to get away. He's shouting something at me, but I'll kind of pretend I can't hear him, and perhaps he'll think I'm just... taking the air up here.

"St Jude. You didn't hear my prayer about other people seeing me down there."

"What? Has somebody found you?"

"Yes, it's bad. I think there's a man in green 'scrubs', I can't quite see properly."

"That's good, isn't it?"

"He's been joined by a dog, I think it's one of those small breeds that bark a lot because it's looking up at me and barking, and its owner has followed to see what the fuss is about. I really do wish this would stop now."

This is even worse though, because they're looking up and I'm convinced they're probably able to see up my skirt. How mortifying, laddered tights and showing off my altogether. I'm going to die of embarrassment if I don't move right now. I'll get off the ledge and stand back onto the drainpipe, that way my skirt can fall back down. OK, it's harder to hold, but I'm feeling less mortified about the ladder and anybody seeing anything.

"Mrs Maslow?" a voice says and I look up. It's the midwife peering out the open window, her mouth an 'oh' of surprise. I look away, then down.

"No, no, no," I cry.

"What? What is it?" Jude is asking me, but for a moment I can't reply because it's too awful for words. I can hear 'his' voice, down there, he's found me. That's the three of them isn't it? Derek, with the doctor down there, and the midwife above, all shouting at me.

41

"I don't think I can pretend I'm not here," I say in a small voice.

"That's good, isn't it? They're there to help you. Not everybody in life gets a safety net do they?"

Jude has not helped me at all. He's lied to me. I peer closely through the window, looking for it, the flame above his head. Where is his light? He must understand how hard it is for me to talk, but it's appalling, because he hasn't listened to a word I've said.

"I prayed to you not to let anybody see me from down below." And then I say, "Put your face to the window Jude, I want to see you."

"My face?"

"Could you—at least—do that for me?" I say and I'm kind of gasping, having a panic attack or something. So then I see his face pressed to the glass. He's got a terrible spotty complexion, but at least he's got a beard, even if it is wispy.

"Can I have my face back now please, this is awfully uncomfortable."

"Yes," I say. I don't know what I was expecting. I'm not thinking right. I twist away and around, but looking down is worse. I can see Derek shouting and waving at me. Shouting that I'm pregnant and to get his wife down, but I can see the silly sausage has his foot squashing the cushion, and he still doesn't get it.

This is awful. I'm small, I shouldn't be seen from there. All I wanted was not to make a fuss. I just wanted to please him, and he was so pleased. All my life I've just wanted to please everybody, is that so much to ask?

"Hello? Irene?"

My hands are trembling but my grip is too hard, too brittle, because I'm angry with him for not listening. Is it me? Of course it's my fault for not praying hard enough, not trying hard enough. *"I promise thee, O blessed Jude, to be ever mindful of this—this—great—favour—* " I stop, because he hasn't helped. No, I've got to keep trying—*"to always honour thee as my special and powerful patron and to"*—I can hear how angry my voice sounds—*"to be ever mindful of this"*—I can't say it—*"this great favour."* I stop. My mother was right, I'm a terrible Catholic, and Jude must be angry with me or something, so instead I say this. Because you have to, don't you.

"Sorry about this, and sorry for bothering you. Please go now. Just forget about it all." I'm dying of embarrassment about the whole thing. I'm so relieved my skirt is down, and I think perhaps they can't see the ladder from that distance after all. The blurriness is good, it feels less real, and it means perhaps they can't see me so well either, like it's not really happening. That's right, isn't it? But I hate the lack of space I have, and never have had any bloody space.

"I'm slipping, I think. Thank you for listening, really, I do apologise, please, thank you. I've got to go now, so I'll say ta ta, please go now, don't wait."

"Wait," Jude says.

He wants me to stay. The bastard who didn't listen to my prayers wants me to stay. Fuck you, St Jude. The awful thought floats out from somewhere. I am appalled. I wish somebody would bloody axe this saint in the head all over again. Or axe him up the arse. Arse. Fuck the whole holy host of them.

"You were my only hope," I say, and then, "Fuck you, St Jude." Out loud it's even better. It goes floating out from my mouth, liberated.

And flies. My voice has got wings! I could fly if I let myself. I could be free. Can I do this? Can I let go?

"You wanted my sodding advice didn't you?" he says.

"I *need* a bloody *miracle*. Now." Again, my voice takes flight and it feels good. Does that mean it would feel good for the rest of me to take flight too?

"Listen. Listen. Don't. If it were me? And I'd faked it and been found out? I'd leg it."

What did he mean?

"Do a runner. I'll help. You haven't killed anybody, nobody's hurt."

"But Derek."

"He'll live. You wanted my advice. Christ, I've known some birds to pretend to be up the jacksy, and make their fellas sweat, or get round security guards at the supermarket by hiding bottles of Daniels and a lamb shank up their skirts. Look, I'll even help. Are you away from the window?"

"What?"

And there's this almighty smash, and this ruddy great big metal pole comes crashing through the window. But Jude doesn't stop there, he smashes again and again, and all the glass comes flying out, landing on my skirt and legs, and peppering down on the small crowd below. I'm thinking perhaps Jude's used his 'shepherd's crook', you know, the staff that saints walk with, because they must put in some miles, although in this day and age they probably get an Uber or something. Or notch up air miles with those cards. Thinking about it, the pole looks like those things you get in hospitals that drips are attached to. A bony hand starts grabbing and twisting out the last remaining shards of glass from the pane, so clearly Jude thinks I could fit through, though

I haven't got a lot of hope, but I have to give it a go. I twist back around from the drainpipe, shaking hard, and it's not pretty, but I lever myself through legs first, skirt shifting up, glass shards mashing into my thighs, snaking tight through the hole, my hips just about make it on the diagonal, so tight it's like being born again, and at the point I realise I'm going to make it through, I have this feeling in my chest, like a starburst. A piece of leftover glass cuts lovingly up my arm, but I don't care, because it's a miracle and I'm through. I'm shaking so hard I slither from the window onto the floor, a breech birth.

I twist and look up, and there He is.

Saint Jude wears a hospital gown and holds a fluids bag in his right hand, and a tube disappears up his sleeve. The black eye and cut lip feature large in his thin pale face, and I marvel at it, because he only looks about eighteen. On one arm he wears in a sling, and the other forearm has a dragon tattoo but without St George, or his horse, and he has awful bruised knuckles. That must have been one fight with the devil, and it doesn't look like he won. But then what do I know about saints, I mean if they have to keep going for centuries, maybe they're a bit like zombies, you know, they don't look good after a while.

Then behind him, I take in the full glory of the men's urinals. God works in mysterious ways.

"Thank you, Jude. You've saved me," I say, and then the waterworks start up again and I can't stop blubbing. I want to hug him, but I'm unable to get off the floor, besides it wouldn't be appro—appro—right to hug a man of his station.

"I've not done anything like that before, you know, saved anybody." He looks down, then coughs and adds, "Well don't hang around you crazy bird, get going. Enjoy your freedom."

"Am I allowed to just go?"

"Yes, seriously, fuck 'em. Can you say that?" he says and stares at me waiting, so I say:

"Fuck 'em." And when it comes out loud, it's dreadful and exhilarating, and I enjoy it and want to say it again, but instead I say:

"Thank you for helping me."

There's a knock on the door, and my heart thumps painfully because I think it's 'him', only a strange beefy voice shouts out:

"Oi, toe rag, this is the longest piss ever. Get your arse out now."

And in walks a policeman swinging handcuffs. I take him in, then take in the cuff around St Jude's ankle.

It appears St Jude is under arrest.

"What're you waiting for Irene, get going. What is it they say, 'God helps those who help themselves?'" Jude says.

"I'll add this to the rap sheet, shall I?" says the copper staring at the smashed window, and then "You OK, Miss? Has he been behaving himself?" Then

47

doing a double take at the door, adds, "Walked through the wrong door?"

I nod vigorously, though he looks suspiciously at me. I know I've only got moments left, so I just keep smiling, and use the wall to push myself up to a standing position. I take off my one shoe and leg it to the door.

"Irene?" Jude calls back.

I turn.

"That felt good. I've never done that before. You know, helped someone. It could be addictive. Thank you," he says. I wave and he does a small wave back.

He's holding his fluids bag like a lamp, and when he smiles he is transfigured. And I swear to you. I swear, as God is my witness, I see it then.

The flame above his head.

I wake in the darkest of hours to hear her high scream. A thick silence rushes in and confuses me. Did she scream? My insomniac mind is awake now and searches for things to focus on, like the skeins of cobweb that hang from the ceiling. I stare uncomprehendingly at a patch of flaking paint and travel through and beyond that, to where the loft heaves with the sheer weight of accumulated belongings. They press down on me. I imagine my daughter's cot folded away in the eaves, next to the baby bottle steriliser, around which so many early parenthood rituals revolved. And the baby-walker stopped in its tracks by amassed boxes of early-years toys, and the primrose bedding that I always meant to give away but never did.

And suitcases that were going nowhere.

I push against the duvet, only to discover I have already pushed the whole thing off, but I still feel its suffocating weight. His old musical collections were still up there, and the stereo, and his copy of Scientific Wonders. Amassed marital detritus left for me to bear. An over-cluttered den.

I hear the red-head's scream long and loud this time. Lucky vixen, with no baggage. A Saturday night tussle. No looking back.

I think I must have fallen asleep but in the morning there's still a scream ringing in my ears. I need to walk. Maybe I'd find her prints. Follow her path out of my nowhere place.

AN UNUSUAL PUB

There is an aroma to the quality of a thing. Like the strawberry tickle of a bottle of Boerl & Kroff Brut, or a pinch of Almas caviar placed on the tongue. It's laughable, but I salivate when I smell the leathered seats of an Aston Martin.

That's how I found you. I smelt you out.

It was a blustery January evening, somewhere forgettable, and because I had followed my nose, not my eyes, I walked straight into a Weatherforks public house without clocking what it was. Not a desert, or a temple, or a hospital, but a purgatorial watering hole of depressing dimensions. Instantly I lost you, as your aroma dissolved in a stench of bleach, beer dregs, and burger fat. Confused, I nearly tripped over a cluster of Lidl plastic bags placed by a table, and was pushed upright by a lady who smelt of cheese and onion crisps and talcum powder. Her thick make-up failed to hide a large hairy mole on her chin. She turned to give me the stink eye but looked away. In the long mirror behind the bar I realised why. My expression was feral. My hunger palpable. I needed to find you. It was unthinkable to be so close and then lose you. I felt like screaming my frustration out until somebody obliged and found you for me. Instead, I pushed my way to the bar and put on my best poker face.

"Got a Lagavulin single malt?"

The bartender didn't waste his scorn, but nodded at a selection of the basest blends. I chose some abomination and he slapped it down onto the puddled bar. I held my breath from its soapy odour and took a sip. I didn't understand anything. Particularly your conjuror's disappearance trick. That was my job. Not that *I'd* hold onto it much longer unless I reeled you in. You had to be in here somewhere. I put the glass down and met the bartender's stare. All mean and guarded. So I stopped with the deep breathing, though I really did need to find a clue fast. I checked my disguise in the mirror behind his bullet-shaped head, but it all looked within the acceptable parameters of normal. In fact, I took some pleasure in the pseudo private investigator garb I'd acquired. High collars looked good on me. So did the hat and belted long coat. You have to allow me some pleasures. I feigned another sip and used the mirror to check out the drab crowd behind me.

And struck lucky. An imperceptible corona gave you away. Bingo.

I walked over to where you hunkered alone in a booth and sat straight down.

"Sorry?" you said, like I'd made a mistake to sit there. Admittedly, you didn't look like I expected you to look. All shaggy haired and a bit hangdog in the face. You nursed a half pint and I marvelled at your bitten nails wrapped around the glass. Was that some kind of stain on your fingers?

"Hey, mate, imagine seeing you here," I said and thrust my hand out. It came to me, it was paint on your fingers. "Didn't we meet at college, you did art didn't you?" I said.

"I didn't go to art college," he said.

"Oh, no that's right," I said and held my head like I'd remember something any moment.

"My little brother got sick and I turned my place down. Ended up working instead to pay for his treatment in the States," he said.

"Yes, of course, I heard that. Great. How is he now?"

"Dead."

"Oh man, I am so sorry," I said.

"Four years now."

"That's tragic, that really is," I said. This was not going well.

"Look I don't mean to be rude or anything but I don't think I know you," he said.

"Listen…"

"Luke," he said.

"That's right, Luke, it was on the tip of my tongue," I said. "But you're a painter right? I got that right didn't I?"

"I'm sorry mate, I'm just…"

"I'm Raum," I said, "but just call me Raoul." I proffered up my hand and he took it. It was all I could do not to sob with relief. It felt soooo good. The smell of him was rich and creamy and sweet like a walking meringue.

"Look Raoul, I don't want to be rude but I'm really not in the mood for company at…"

"Why's that Luke? What's happened?" I said, all concerned. I took off my hat, pulled into him across the table, and made myself look comfortable.

"Listen, I really don't want to…" he said and wiped his face with his hand.

"Seriously Luke, I want to help I really do. For old time's sake," I said. He snorted at that, like I was taking the mickey.

"You can't. Nobody can." I saw his jaw clench as he looked away. Bad then.

"How do you know?" I asked.

"Because it's the kind of thing that can't be fixed easily," he said and I could hear the impatience in his tone like I was gonna lose him.

"What, is your mother sick? Your father?" I asked, all soft like. He looked at me strangely.

"Dad's been gone for ten years mate, are you having a laugh?" He looked around as if he expected someone to be filming the prank with their phone. Oh I couldn't lose him, I simply couldn't. If I lost this one then I lost my job forever and that didn't bear thinking about because it was more than a job, it was my absolute life. Things had not been good lately. It won't surprise you to know that automation has had a lot to do with that. Algorithms could now replicate centuries worth of finely honed instincts. Bots could check the sites people visited, the purchases they made, contacts they kept and then when they'd identified the ripe ones? Harvested them. How could bots tell? They couldn't smell the ripeness of a quality soul like I could. There were not many of us freelancers left now.

"What if I said I could fix it, whatever it is," I said. I knew I must've looked a bit wild, desperate even, but what could I do? I had to put it out there and keep him talking.

"I don't think you can get my woman to love me and come back, can you mate." he said.

"What, she must be mad not to love you," I said and meant it, and added, "a kind man like you? A compassionate man? Are you sure she doesn't love you anymore?" Maybe there was something genuine in my voice because he hesitated.

"I don't even know you, mate," he said and tipped back the last of his drink.

"Aren't those the best conversations? Where you don't have to worry about another person's opinion? Think of me like, a counsellor. We might never meet again, so what have you got to lose?"

"What, you're my guardian angel are you? Sent to look after me?" he said and laughed. I laughed too at that, because it was funny.

"So what do I do then, mate?" he asked, "I mean I understand, I really do. I think she'd be better off without me too. I have no money, no prospects. My art sucks."

"Surely not."

"Do you want to buy a painting? Now that would help me out. She might think differently if I had some money." He looked at me all hopeful like. I smiled back. I needed to proceed cautiously here.

"That's not quite what I'd like to buy," I said, "But I have a proposition for you." I pushed my vile whisky over to him and he stared at it.

"Thanks. I don't usually," he said and took the glass. He necked a swig cautiously like the lightweight he was.

"There is, however, something I do want to buy that you have," I said.

"Oh really?" he said and sat up straighter.

"But first, what would you say if I said I could get your girl to love you?" I said. He laughed but it looked like he wanted to cry, and he slumped back down again, the whisky nursed between his ragged hands.

"I don't think you understand how much I love her. I've always felt things deeply. I was the sort of kid who couldn't watch sad or scary movies. I was devastated when my dog Milo died. And don't even get me started on my kid brother's fight with leukaemia. It never gets any easier and every cruelty or loss cuts at me. I can't watch news of war or famine or fire. If I see a mum clip her kiddie's ear in the street, I'm like, in bits. The only thing that's ever helped me has been my painting. It eases the pain. Sorry, I'm talking too much. But what I'm saying is you can't imagine how hard I fell for this girl. It was like special."

"Yes, I see." And I did. I was probably one of only a handful of Watchers left who did understand what it was he felt. Passion or ecstasy seemed to be words that belonged now to a different era. The depth of a feeling for a person or object. I certainly felt that desire myself. Because the rarer an item is, the more valuable it becomes. Like the occasional flowering of a Youtan Poluo, or the possession of Giacometti's L'Homme au doigt, or to hear a 1950s Gibson Moderne played, it was the very rarity of these items that rendered them all the more desired, more coveted. More valuable.

Sometimes these things come along only once in a century. And I had found in you the most singular of things—a pure soul.

"Was it metaphorical what you said about helping me earlier? Are you like in insurance or something?" he asked.

"You could say I'm in insurance," I said.

"What do you do?"

"I—travel a lot. I do freelance. Though automation is crucifying me," I said and laughed but he just nodded, so I carried on. "Countries moan about migration taking jobs away, but believe me, it's automation. I used to think what I did was unique and irreplaceable, but it seems there's nothing that can't be replicated. To be honest, unless I get a sale soon my boss is going to—sack me, let's say."

"That's rough," he said.

"He's vicious. I promised him results months—years ago. I've been expecting termination for weeks. It used to be that my business was more like human research. I was called a Watcher. But there's been so many redundancies that I've been forced to take on others' jobs, so now I'm like 'hands on', you know? Not just doing the private detective work, you could say, but making the—sale too. Bringing people in."

He nodded and took another sip.

"Is there anything I can do to help?" he said.

"Yes, there is actually. Can I ask you, do you carry a Donor Card?" I said.

"Yes, of course."

"What for? Your kidneys? Your eyes? Your heart?" I asked.

"Everything. It would be nice to think I'd be of use to somebody if I died." He smiled and made circles with his glass on the table.

"Exactly. Exactly," I said. Around us, the pub had got busier and as the noise increased I found I shouted this a little too excitedly. "Well, think about my—our—scheme in the same way as donating your heart," I said, then leant in close to him and whispered, "Only it's your soul you are donating."

"Soul? Donating?" he asked.

"Exchanging. It's not like you walk away empty handed from this. It's a win-win situation. You think you've lost your girl. You think that's the kind of thing somebody else can't fix for you, but you're wrong. With ordinary souls such as hers, there's always leverage—money, a nice house, a good job, no job, babies. There are things we can offer your girl that will have her running back to you in super quick time. It is only pure souls, like you, that live conscious lives, that take choices seriously, the rest of you poor mortals stumble around like puppets. Pull the strings and you move."

"How did you know that? That I'm so conscious of the consequences of what I do all the time?" he whispered back.

"Because I understand, I really do," I said and patted his hand. I wouldn't say I felt remorse for what I was doing, and what I knew would become of him, but I felt something close as I said:

"Do you want this girl to love you?"

"Yes, but not by the means you're describing," he countered.

"Look, she just needs a little persuasion to start with but then she genuinely would. You have a capacity to love so it's easier for others to follow that algorithm." I used that hated word.

"Are you talking about me selling my soul and in exchange you will get my girl to love me?" he stated.

"Bingo."

He sat back and finished the whiskey in one go.

"What would happen to it?" he asked.

"What?"

"My soul."

"Does it matter?" I said.

"Would it be sitting in a cabinet somewhere? Or would my life change? What should I expect?" He laughed then, like he thought I was joking.

"Nothing. A full and meaningful life. You're happy, she's happy, I'm happy. Sounds good right?"

He looked around again as if to spot the others in on the prank, then looked back and stared into the depths of me. I had no doubt my fate balanced between his brittle nailed hands. I could do nothing but—pray. I know, but before my fall it used to work and old habits die hard.

"And afterwards?"

I could tell from his tone that he was humouring me, but shrugged and asked him:

"Does it matter what happens afterwards?"

"This is a joke right?" he said.

"Look, I'm not some cowboy here, you know. There's a contract you can read and sign. All legal and legitimate." I looked him straight in the eye.

"Look, sorry, no," he said.

"Listen, I'm a professional with centuries of experience. From a long line of Grigori who serve the one true—Boss. To you, your soul is a burden, but to my boss it would be a thing of beauty..." I don't add

61

that my boss would delight in it, play with it, and over the long years come to take it on an intricate journey from purity to corruption. Instead I added:

"He desires exquisite things."

The noise intensified around us as the Saturday crowd warmed into their usual excesses. Yet in the middle of that hubbub, our stillness was stretched to breaking point. I was frozen with terror, unable to contemplate losing such a thing of beauty. To explain a little about the nature of souls, imagine how you react when a driver cuts you up. Or your dad gives you a slap. Or somebody scams money out of your account. Now imagine that you always consciously think, then base your reactions to those scenarios only on what would be for the greater good? Imagine looking down the line of your life and making decisions not on how you felt at that moment, or what was the easiest thing to do, but on what consequences were attached to each decision. Now think about how many of those decisions you make in a lifetime. It's massive. A pure soul is a mathematical singularity. A beautiful sum. And I was asking him now to make a *wrong* decision.

"Yes, okay, I'll do it," he said. For a moment I was floored by the quick assent. Then a wave of sheer elation hit me and I rocked back in my seat. This was too easy. I sniffed and caught a whiff now of a base note to his silky aroma. The slightest of flaws. It was always going to be impossible to reel him in untainted, but nevertheless somewhere in that complete high I felt something else. Disappointment? It was always about the fall with the Big Guy. The journey. He wasn't really interested in those souls that corrupted easily, the naturally evil, because where was the challenge in that? No, it was those souls that were destined upstairs that interested him. They were the real wins. I wondered, if your average Joe realised there was no redemption from sins, would he sin quite so easily? Because here's the thing. The Guy upstairs doesn't forgive so easily. Forget your New Testament flannel, he was an Old Testament God. Always had been. And contradictory too. You could say that both Him Upstairs and the Boss were similar contrary creatures. It was ulcer inducing.

"Though I want to see this contract." Luke jabbed his finger onto the sticky table and I nodded and patted my pockets. Careful Raum, I thought, it's not a done deal yet. I pulled out the contract, undid the string and rolled the parchment as flat as it would go. He placed his hand and traced the aged writing with his finger in wonderment.

"I think I'm going to need a drink for this. Would you mind?" he said. He looked a funny colour, like he realised this could actually be for real, so I got up. I damped down my irritation, a desire to shout at him to just sign and be done with it. Instead I said:

"Don't go away okay. Stay right there."

"I don't have a pen," he called out as I backed into the crowd and towards the bar.

"No problem, no problem, I'll get a pen too," I said. Anything. Because this would mean my reprieve. And no severance. Severance of limbs, eyes and organs. Instead of slow, profound and yawning suffering, I could expect to idle away years of pleasurable excess. I pushed my way to the bar and turned back, but I couldn't see him.

"Give me two whiskeys and a pen," I said as the barman walked by. I swore he saw me, but Bullethead made a big show of serving the oik beside me.

"Look, give me two whiskeys and a pen. I'm in a hurry," I shouted into his face, but he ignored me and pulled the oik's pint in slow time. Sometimes hell is a slow bar. I turned around and tried to see if Luke was still there but the crushed assemblage of drinkers had closed in around him. Finally, Bullethead eyed me up and oh-so-slowly dispensed the whiskey.

"And a pen. A pen."

The man shrugged his shoulders and waited for his payment, which I took to mean no pen. The sale of a lifetime and no pen? You couldn't make this up. I scanned the pub again, and spotted the woman from earlier as she traced the edge of her lips with a lip pencil. I pinched the two whiskeys in one hand with my fingers and staggered back, then effected a nudge as I passed her. Bits of make-up clattered from her open bag to the damp and sweated floor beneath and I ducked down and grabbed at a rolling eye pencil. For a moment I eyed her shocked face at floor level as she ducked down and then scrabbled up. The eye pencil would have to do. Time was of the essence now. My empty chest beat like there was a real heart in there, because I still couldn't see Luke. Suddenly I spotted my mark and felt a deep wash of relief. There he was, talking to himself of all things. No. Not to himself, because some stranger now sat opposite.

"Hey," I cried out and pushed through the crowd to the table. The man turned.

It was Vassago.

"What're you doing here? Go away, he's mine," I said and restrained myself from pushing him aside. Vassago was taller than me and was dressed in a smart blue suit. He stood up and proffered his hand.

"Is that any way to treat a friend, Raum?" Vassago's smile held no warmth as he clasped my hand in the two of his meaty fists and shook it against my will.

"This is—my—friend." I released my bruised hand to point emphatically at Luke.

"It's okay Raoul, he's explained that you work for the same firm," Luke said and held up a tablet on which I could see a neatly typed identical contract.

"But you were going to sign *my* contract," I replied. I felt faint and sweaty, and watched as the pub twisted and corkscrewed around me. I was worse than dead if I lost him now, so I turned on Vassago. "You can't just walk in here and steal him." I couldn't help it, my eyes flashed red. It was difficult to control the rage that coursed through me.

"Hey, let's keep this professional shall we?" Vassago said, though his gaze was shot with crimson too and the air crackled with the smell of sulphur.

"Look, I don't want to cause trouble. Perhaps I should go," Luke said and began to rise from his seat.

"No," we cried out in unison and my hand shot up to Luke's shoulder as Vassago grabbed his arm.

"I really don't want to cause trouble," Luke persisted and I realised we would both lose him so I said:

"Listen, it's just a misunderstanding. Let me have a private word here with my colleague and we'll sort it out. Just, drink your drink okay? And don't move. Promise?"

"Promise," he said.

"Good." I grabbed Vassago by the sleeve and practically hauled him out of the chair, and together we pushed through the crowd. Loud music crested across shouted conversations and the crowd jostled each other. Faces turned and stared at us, and I was reminded of a Hieronymus Bosch painting. I hate being amongst the rabble and have some bad memories of mobs. I didn't know where to go for this conversation, so I headed to the gents with my hand firmly on Vassago's arm.

"Maybe we could split him," Vassago said.

"Split him? It'd be like splitting a baby—neither of us would gain. No, he's mine," I insisted.

"Oi, you." A weasel of a man pressed his hand into my chest and stopped my progress. "Did you interfere with my Missus?" The man said.

"I don't know what you're talking about," I said and went to side step the idiot. A female voice behind him cried out, "That's him," and I clocked the hairy-moled woman whose eye pencil still nestled in my pocket.

"Problem Raum? Perhaps I should let you sort this out," Vassago said and I felt him try to slip out of my grip. I pulled back determined not to let go, just as the oik grabbed my other arm and pulled at me too. For a moment the three of us struggled like some tango-ing trio, and a circle of space emerged on the heaving pub floor. Cries of 'Watch it', 'Push off' and 'Easy, easy,' emanated from the uniformly ugly clientele.

"Let go of me," Vassago said.

"I'm not holding you," the oik replied.

"No, him," Vassago said and pointed at me.

"Nasty piece of work you are, aren't you? Let's settle this outside," the weasel-like fellow said and tried to pull me towards the door and I felt my grip of Vassago yanked to breaking point. One last shove and the oik shoved me back and into a table. Pints toppled and a cry went up from the three rugby players who now found their laps full of beer. The burliest specimen rose up in front of me, just as I saw Vassago push his way back through the crowd. Suddenly a fist flew at me and I ducked. Above me the oik had taken the full force of the blow and had staggered back into a stag party beside the bar. They in turn pushed him back into the three rugby players and then I am honestly not sure what happened, but punches started to fly, and I dropped down. Somebody tripped over me, but hands and knees pumping, I scrabbled around the table legs and back in what I thought was the direction of Vassago. Behind me screams sang out as did the sound of tables being overturned. I rose up, but too soon, because in front of me stood Bullethead.

"I knew you were trouble," he said in a gravelled voice, then smiled as he punched me square on the nose. I heard bone crunch and staggered back and over an upturned table. I rolled awkwardly and put my left hand to the wreckage of my nose to stem the streaming blood. Through rose tinted vision, I clocked Bullethead's foot hover over my supporting hand, then he ground my fingers into the floor. Pain took my breath away, as I looked up into his mashed mistake of a face. Beyond the brute, I caught a glimpse of Vassago who must have hesitated, keen no doubt to see me get a pasting. Suddenly the pain let up, as Bullethead was nudged off centre by a fracas beside him. As my fingers were released I scrabbled up and barrelled forwards towards the sadist. At the last minute though, I swerved and ran into Vassago full pelt. As the pair of us went down, we took those behind us with us, like ten pins. I landed heavily and for a moment my eyesight swam, but I held to what I thought was Vassago's suit. As my vision cleared I realised I held the front of the hairy-moled woman's blouse and she let rip with an almighty scream. There was a pause as her friends registered the assault then they came at me from all sides like a rugby scrum.

I went down in a pile of bodies, and I am honestly not sure what happened for the next few minutes, but suffice to say somehow I crawled out. This time I didn't attempt to get up until I was practically at Luke's table, then used the adjacent table to lever myself up. Was that Vassago by Luke's side? It couldn't be because Luke was holding to somebody as if protecting them from the chaos around.

"Luke. There you are. Sorry. So Sorry, but if we could please just..." I shoved the contract into his chest and proffered up the eye pencil in my broken fingers. I sniffed hard to try and hoover up some of the blood from my busted nose.

"Raoul. It's okay, it's okay now. I don't need your help," Luke said and smiled a smile of such sweetness that cherubims and seraphims should have blown their golden trumpets in delight. Behind me I heard Vassago stagger forwards and stop to rest on my shoulder. His shirt had been ripped from the front of his chest and a nasty bruise blossomed on his cheekbone. I looked to where Luke gazed and froze.

"This is her. This is my Belinda," Luke said.

"It's Belial," Vassago whispered beside me.

"She's come back to me," Luke said, "Only a lover's tiff after all. She just wanted proof of my love, that's all." Luke sobbed the words out, and beside him Belial smiled like the vixen she was and nestled into his side.

"And you can show me proof, Luke," she said. "Let's go somewhere quiet now. Then I can get you to sign my very own special contract." She kissed him oh so sweetly on the lips and saw the look of him. Bewitched. Lost. I knew I was beat. That she-devil must have been working him for months.

"Excuse us boys," she said and her crimson eyes flashed as she pouted at us and pushed past. I realised I was mumbling under my breath, "No, please, please, please," but what was the point? Luke followed behind her, obedient as a lamb to the slaughter, and I knew I'd lost.

"What do you think He'll do to us?" Vassago said and turned to me, big tear-stains visible in his fallen angel's eyes.

"I hope it doesn't involve vomit, I hate vomit," I said.

"Or animals," he said and I could feel his trembling beside me. Or was that me trembling? The sounds of the vicious brawl continued around us so I could hardly hear him.

70

"Perhaps he's got bigger fish to fry," I said and together we shouldered our way through the mob and limped towards the door.

"Or perhaps we made him laugh. He has a sick sense of humour," Vassago said.

"Just so long as the punishment isn't subtle. His subtlety is worse than his cruelty," I whispered as I pushed open the door arm-in-arm with my frenemy. I needed fresh air.

We walked out.

And walked straight back into the Weatherforks. The same pub. Only the crowd were a little wilder, and an old man was lying on the floor in a puddle of vomit. And the bulletheaded barman was biting into an underage teenager's hand. No, this wasn't happening. We stumbled back and out of the same door again.

And entered straight back into the same pub.

Only the Hieronymus Bosch multitude looked wilder still. The oik of earlier was now repeatedly bashing an old woman over the head with her own Lidl grocery bag, whilst a man loosed his vicious Alsatian to tear at the limbs of a group of brawlers. The scrum of rugby players had grown pig-like faces and were forcing a bottle of spirits down the neck of a pregnant woman, whilst the hairy-moled woman groped members of the stag party. The row of spirit bottles at the back of the bar now resembled teeth in a deep cavernous maw. Overwhelmed by the sheer stench of the place, I sank to my knees.

The Boss was joking with us. Had manifested a fresh new Hell.

Trapped on a Saturday night in a Weatherforks for all of eternity.

The night is hot and my bedroom window is thrown wide open. She is a mother now. Out there I hear her familiar chitter and new answering squeals with a mixture of wonder and irritation. More pilfered bins and ravaged debris. No, no that's not right, what were the facts I read about an urban fox's diet? But my fogged brain can't be bothered to file through facts and prefers to grasp at fictions. Maybe it's her profound difference, her alienness that means I can impose anything I like on her. I know when I go fox walking in my city it's easier to weave stories around strangers.

I turn over and settle onto my good side, determined to hunt down, pursue and overpower my broken sleep. I just want to be left alone now and wish she'd go, leave, and get out of my city for good. Because if she would just go away perhaps I wouldn't feel so goddamn restless.

I drift asleep and she drags a broken bag of chaos through my dreams.

THE BACK GARDEN

My living room is small, cramped, and hot. The laptop sits low on the desk and my chair is too high so I'm all ugly elbows and knees as I type. Precious cool air teases at me through an inch gap in the broken sash window and if it were not for the overgrown ivy I would be able to see the back garden.

But not now, I'm too busy going mad.

"I'm making an insect castle," Jack says. He's waiting for me to turn and give him my attention, but I keep typing. The sales report is due in twenty minutes, and three contracts are still outstanding.

"It's got a drawbridge."

I hear him swing on the door handle, which he's not supposed to do, and I turn.

"Jack, don't swing."

I look back at the nonsense I've written. Will they take my 'July Employee Award' back if they find out? Fire me, more like. I was ready to close the deals properly this morning, only I got the call from Miss Sing, Jack's reception class teacher, asking me to pick up him up. A cold, she'd said, though I hadn't heard Jack sniffle once. Who gets a cold in high summer?

"Do you want to see it?" Jack comes close, leans into me and drapes his hot clammy arms over my skirt. He wants to get on my lap, but I close the gap between my lap and the desk.

"No." It comes out too firm, and I see his face fall and feel a frisson of fear that he's going to have a meltdown.

"Why don't you build the walls higher? Does it have turrets?" I sing song at him. Jack searches my face and looks hopeful.

"I could build them higher," he breaks off and runs out. Yes, I can still do this. Make the calls, get these signed, and finish the report. I need this job, I have to pay the mortgage arrears on this airless flat, now.

"Then you can come and see," Jack adds. My fingers are already flying over the keyboard when I hear the email ping and flip screens. Harcrofts. Querying the tie in period. Want to exercise their right to the fourteen-day cool off. Under the oppressive heat, I am quite cold. I can't seem to stop myself clenching and unclenching my hands, frozen into inaction. My mobile lights up with my boss's number and my heart turns a couple of somersaults as I let it go to voicemail.

"It's ready, Mum."

Jack's back.

"Not now."

"You promised," he wails.

"Don't you understand, I'm busy," I yell. His face reddens, his eyes fill with tears, before he kicks the door hard and flies out howling. I hesitate. Even then. But I can hear him from here, and imagine Mrs Watson peering out the nets at my crying child in the garden. Goddammit. I get up so hard the chair flies back and a flurry of papers slip off the desk. Perhaps I can still calm him down and do this. I have to.

The strident call of my mobile follows me. I clench my teeth and ignore it.

Lush and overgrown, the garden cannot hide his sobs. I walk across the yellowed square of bare lawn, then push through a conspiracy of hedge and heavy scented honeysuckle, before spotting Jack flat on his belly under the apple tree. Dusty earth sticks to his sweaty legs and the back of his shorts. It's hard to look at the garden as anything other than a long to-do list, and I fight my instinct now to deal with the dirt on Jack's shorts, rather than his tears. When had everything in my life morphed into work?

"Is that the insect castle?" I say.

"It's a hotel," he shouts, turning his red face to me. How am I supposed to make him understand that if I get fired, this town doesn't *have* jobs, then I'd lose the flat, then we'd have to move, and if I didn't make it so goddamn easy for his dad, the bastard wouldn't bother with contact with Jack. In other words, it all collapses. I hug myself and try to contain the answering wave of anger.

The mobile rings again, and this time I flip the mute on and tread closer, then bend down to see the hotel.

Pieces of twig and small leaves make the walls. A bigger dock leaf, the drawbridge. His hotel guests, ants and a woodlouse, meander over their room walls and wander away.

"Don't. You're disturbing them," he says and pulls up the drawbridge leaf. My head is screaming at me to get back up and go inside and try to salvage something from the work disaster, yet I find myself crouching lower.

"Hey, this could be the bed," Jack says, and takes my mobile and wedges it in the dry earth. I grit my teeth and let him. A petal is stretched across for the blanket.

It's a marvel it even stands as the simplest of breezes will have the whole thing toppling down. He hovers a too large twig precariously over the wall.

"Stop. It'll collapse!" I say.

"Mum," he says, like I'm the child, "then we just build it again."

Let it collapse and build again. It's obvious.

Hours later, our newer, bigger Hotel Batman has shoe walls, paper carpets, a gym for the toy soldiers, twig corridors, and dock leaf doors.

And when the rose petal blanket vibrates and through its pink light I see revealed the boss's number on my buried mobile? I don't answer.

I can do this now. I can let it fall apart.

Across the slicked darkness of the canal we square up. I want to ask what she's doing there at the canal at this hour, but she stares her question back first. What? I ask, you want to know my story? There's nothing to tell. I'm a single mum like you. Just struggling at the moment. Feeling lost in the familiar. Tired of being on the outside, but not wanting to be on the inside either, you know that one? But there's nothing more, really.

But her stare is so bold it makes me angry. She has no respect for appropriate etiquette, let alone ownership. Her kind have invaded us, I say to the vixen in my head. At least I abide by the rules.

How far does that get you, she asks. She sniffs the air as if searching for other human smells that may be part of me. Only there aren't any. She licks the tip of her tongue over her sharp nose as if to settle into conversation. What will her opener be? 'I'll tell you a bit of my story, and then perhaps you can tell me yours?'

I say nothing and she blinks back. Her orange eyes tell her story, of a den, near a village, but that village turned into a town. And wood was swapped for brick, and then an army of axes, diggers and cranes dug deep into her earth, her dens, as we pushed our cities into the skies. Then we persisted, thrust ourselves into her world, to hunt down her kind. This is what her eyes tell me.

But she's only a fox and who trusts a fox's story.

BY THE CANAL

6am Friday. I don't mean to slam the front door, it just happens. A morning run fills me with this fierce energy and I don't know my own strength. I take off my soaked trainers in the hall and wait to hear her holler and complain, and moan and nag, nag, nag about the slam. It's always the little things that have her riled and up in arms, but that's redheads for you. The house sits in silence, so I figure she must be out, or in the garden, and leap up the stairs two at a time. I let the shower run for three whole minutes, whilst I strip off my sodden running gear, plenty time to let the stupid boiler warm up, then I duck into the shower.

"No," I bellow, engulfed with a stone cold downpour. I can't believe the cow has used up all the hot water.

"Sophie. Sophie." There's still no answer and I wonder if she's there but ignoring me. Giving me the cold treatment. I'll show her how tough I am, I think, and stand, snorting like a bull, letting the freezing water do its job, till I feel strangely calm and the heat's taken out of me. OK, I get it, I know she's right. I've always been pig-headed and intent on getting my own way. Like insisting we buy this stupid leaking house with its crappy plumbing. My mum was always on my case about it, like, lighten up and see her side of things. You know what this is really about, don't you son? Nesting. It's about her wanting the baby. The baby. Always the baby. That's what she really wants. Yes, yes, yes, YES. The anger boils back up again, and I imagine steam coming off the bitter-cold water. OK, I'll have it out with her, only, keep calm this time.

I step out of the shower, change into my work clothes then skip down the stairs, feeling the carpet cleave to my damp feet. I open the kitchen door and feel a frisson of shock, because she's there after all, at the table with her back to me, displaying her power of red hair. The witch. I watch for a moment as she pushes her spoon around the still full cereal bowl. She's not eating? Is she feeling sick, nauseous? Could this be the reason for her silences? Well, you would think that would put a smile on her face. Is there no pleasing the woman? No, I'm keeping calm this time.

I wait for her to say something. I wait for me to say something, but instead there's this silence, and all the time a drip, drip, drip of the kitchen tap.

"Why'd you come back?" she says. "Why'd you bloody well come back?" She doesn't bother to turn and face me. So, I figure she's not pregnant then, but why do I get it in the neck? Instantly my anger rises, and I can't hold it.

"Some loving wife you are. Ignore me would you?" I say and take the cupboard door handle and bang it hard, again and again.

"I—don't—have—to—put—up—with—this."

I slam out the rhythm, but she doesn't even flinch. Alright then, I'm going to scare her and not come back tonight. That'll teach her.

I stride down the corridor, shove my sockless wet feet into my trainers and slam the front door so hard it shakes in its hinges. She can worry herself sick, call her parents and the bloody police again, see if I care.

5.30am Saturday. I'm digging my heels in up Marriot Hill and going hard for the burn, because there's the marathon to think of and its only three weeks off. As I turn onto the path through the park gates, I feel this nervous energy, because I'm already thinking it leads to the canal. I hate water, particularly deep, dark oily water, where you can't see the bottom, but it's good to push yourself and keep 'facing your demons' as my old Dad would've said.

Besides, I know every step is bringing me closer to her. I was as good as my word and didn't go back home last night, so I've been away long enough that she'll have softened by now and be glad to see me. It'll be like the old days when we'd argue yet afterwards her love would be strawberry sweet. I love that woman and when I get back things are going to be different.

I'm going well, and feeling the flow. I twist down the steel steps that lead to the walkway that runs beside the canal, but then things go wrong. There's these two dirty yobs who've got their cycles lying there blocking the path, and they're lounging all casual like on the grass, but I'm not buying it, and if they think they're scaring me, they've got another think coming, because you've got to show these people.

"Get out of the way." I don't stop running, just jump the bikes, because I'm scared, I'm scared they'll throw me in the canal, and I don't know where the thought comes from, but that's it. I stumble as I land, and I, I—

—I run... I run through the fear, I hate being scared, and prefer the fury that rises in me, enabling me to dig in my heels, pump my arms and channel it. I push myself hard till I outrun the thought and leave it behind. Then I hit my street where my house is and my wife sits waiting for me. I'm full of rage, and know I've got to get rid of it before I get home.

But I burst through that front door at full pelt, feeling the fury pump through my body, soaking wet once more with sweat. I don't head for the shower but instead go straight into the kitchen, because I know she'll be there. I bet she hasn't had any sleep for the worry of me, and when I open the door I feel a moment's satisfaction at the state of her, all pale and ill-looking.

"Why'd you come back?" she sighs.

"Why d'you think, you stupid cow," I say. Because it's so good to feel her soften, to know I can win her back from anger to love. Stroke her cheek, feel the slimness of her waist and pull her to me.

"Why d'you always come back?" She says again, but this time it really annoys me.

"Why, why, why. Because it's not fair is it?" I snatch the photo of me sitting there in front of her on the table. It's the one where I'm punching the air, and she's run up to hug me as I've come over the line at my first London Marathon back in '13. I love that photo.

"I'm supposed to run that marathon again in three weeks," I say, and raise the photo high so I can smash it down into pieces and get a reaction. Something out of her. Only it doesn't happen. I swallow hard. I have to try to get through.

"I know, I know, I'm supposed to be fixing this stupid house up too. And busting my ass so we can get another bigger one. And fill it with the kids you want, and I want. There's so much I should be doing. I should be taking you and making love to you, right now. I should be there with you, at the birth of my first child, and second, and third. Because I love you and everything that we were together."

I sit down heavily then, and rest my head on the table, and a patch of wetness appears, and all the time there's that drip, drip, drip of the ruddy tap that's still not fixed, and it's worked its way into my brain, but I'm not through talking.

"I know, Sophie. I hate that you think about what happened all the time. It was you who had to stare at my dead face and identify me. I hate it that I didn't have the chance to mess us up, because it was taken from me. I bet my dad's having a laugh up there in heaven at that one. Because I'm a sissy who couldn't swim."

She ignores me, instead reaches for the wine bottle and pours a glass, like she always does, and there's this haunted look, but I can't, I can't.

"You leave me then. You leave—me," I shout in her face, though I want to kiss it.

But I know she won't.

A silence closes in then and I know I have to leave but I don't know if I've got the strength. I sit there instead, listening to the drip, drip, drip of the tap, till it's got me gritting my teeth in rage, so I go over to the sink and twist the tap handles hard in frustration.

Behind me she gets up, and for a moment I think she's going to hug my back, but instead she pulls a tea towel from the oven door handle and lets it drop into a puddle beneath my chair.

I hate this house. It smells like a sewer.

6am Sunday. Not much farther now. These past months, I know I've been pushing myself too hard, running always running. I've had to keep going, thinking if I run fast enough I'll get back to her. Pretty dumb, huh. But it's not much farther now. In fact, I'm even taking it easy as I skip down the steps towards the canal, knees and elbows swinging. I have a memory now that stops me thinking about the approaching dark water. I think of how she looked last Christmas when she wore the black dress with the low back, and her long, red rope of hair hung against the whiteness of her skin, and how she turned and smiled at me, with those red, red lips of hers, and her marvellous temper was sheathed in velvet. It was always the little things that left her up in arms, but the big things? We were so solid, we loved each other—End Of. A big, raw, ugly-beautiful thing no one else understood.

I stop at the bottom of the steps, hold to the central post, and stretch my calf muscles, left leg first, then right. And as I look up and along the path, I see her coming. She looks small in her black trench coat, tied tight, and unsteady on her heels. She raises her arm. Has she really seen me? I see myself through her eyes; a dumb ox of a man, thinking he has to run hard up against something, and all the time all I had to do was wait.

I start to walk towards her. She stands at the edge of the canal, in the exact same spot where I—where I. She lowers her arm then, and I see her knees buckle, her red lips form an 'o' of surprise, and I start towards her, realisation dawning, that I never did need to run so hard.

Because she's coming to me.

Is this the only way? I run towards her, but she hits the surface whilst I'm still three steps away. Do I want this for her? No, but I'm a bloody selfish bastard and if this is the only way I can have her again, then so be it. But I can't let her face the horror alone, so I don't allow myself to think, but jump too.

I sink instantly. Something, some weed, or her hair perhaps, slips silkily across my ankles, but I'm panicking, thrashing around, the sensation no better than the first time it happened. Stupidly I hold onto my breath, though I have none. Where is she? Everything will be alright if I can only hold her again, show her she is not alone, be with her when she needs me. I can be strong if she is weak.

A hand grabs my ankle, then another, and I panic even though I know it must be her. We are thrashing and grabbing each other, in an embrace of agony not ecstasy, and I feel her, using my body, pressing me down, seeking to rise once more. No, no, doesn't she love me? But survival is stronger than love surely. I should let her go and I hate myself, but I hold her anyway. Does she feel me, can she feel me?

The fight goes out of her, and I feel her arms willingly enfold me, and the distance between us dissolves and I am pressed up against her body, and she against mine.

We sink. Her glorious hair drifting up and around her white face, her green eyes wide open, and staring clearly at me now. I have pushed myself hard to get to her, but at last I feel her mouth on mine, as her final breath is released in a struggle of air bubbles between our lips.

We are together once more, forever.

And that's when I feel the gentle swell of her belly. Pregnant?

Suddenly I'm clutching at her soft and slippery body. I kick my legs and try to rise. Try to force my non-existent breath back into her mouth. But she slips through my arms and sinks.

She sinks.

Twisting and grappling, we descend to the bottom of the canal where the slow current drags us through the detritus of life. There is mud on her face, and she has lost her shoe. I hold to her coat carefully as if I could wrap her up, but she is lost and so am I. The canal receives my tears, eyes blind in the black body of water.

3am echoes with emptiness. The main road is

deserted, so she is easy to spot. She is an orange animal bathed in orange street-light. I see her eyes winking on and off as she turns her head this way and that. This is risky though, being so close to her main predator. Us in our cars. Perhaps her cubs are hungry, perhaps she's desperate. Is there nowhere she wouldn't go? Is this what happens when you know no boundaries, that you are prepared to go anywhere? I remind myself she is one in a long line of survivors that have 'played chicken' across our network of death roads. She agrees and crosses the road without a glance then trots towards the nicer end of town, no doubt in search of better quality leftovers.

Then she sees me and stops. 'And what are you doing out here at this hour', she asks? It's my turn to bristle under that direct stare, because I am not part of her story collection. I am not trapped here, I could leave anytime I like. Perhaps I'll take a holiday.

It is me that walks away first this time...

JUST ANOTHER CITY

Eva sinks into the overfriendly embrace of an ageing armchair, stretches her tired body, and indulges in the pleasure of the view from her 4th floor window at the Havana Libre Hotel. The window is built to the same large proportions as the rest of the room and stretches across the entirety of the wall's width.

"Lord, look at my hair. What a chunky cut they gave me, I can't do a thing with it," Jill calls out to Eva. Eva turns briefly to Jill, her 'roomie' of eight days in Cuba, and watches as she critiques her bouffant in a grandiose arched mirror. She doesn't know how Jill wants it to look, but it looks fine to her. When Eva turns back to stare out of the window, a peppermint green 1959 Buick has drawn up to park outside a primary school painted in Navaho Orange. A bright pink Cadillac on the opposite side of the road draws alongside, elbows are rested on the windows then, as conversation ensues between the two drivers. A swirl of ice cream pastels.

"I really will have to do something about my wrinkles when I get back. A new regime perhaps," Jill calls out. Eva sighs. For eight whole days Jill has

95

maintained a running commentary on her hair, clothes, shoes, nails, skin, face, and body. For the first few days, Eva had found she was clenching her teeth in irritation, wondering what to say to stop the obsessive focus. But now?

She turns back to Havana.

The street below displays a disparate mix of architectural styles. The delicate traceries of ironwork on turn of the century verandas nuzzle next to the sleek lines of peeling white art deco facades. Which in turn, share shoulder room with brash chunky '50s concrete apartment blocks. They've patched up their differences now, and stand united in shared decay.

"I wonder if I should wear the black dress tonight, what do you think?" Jill asks, the question rhetorical, as she disappears into the bathroom. Eva is left to marvel at the peeling white art deco apartment opposite, and trace its pleasantly curling edge to the corner wall. On the roof, various stubby plants have seized their opportunity to take root in the crumbling concrete, some cascading flamboyantly over the edge to the front of the building.

"I don't know why I haven't lost any weight yet," Jill's voice filters back. Then louder. "What do you think Eva?" Eva is forced to turn, and assesses Jill as she stands there holding a blue dress up by its hanger for inspection. Her large laced black underwear contrasts with puckered white flesh, the scar from her recent hip operation a soft red.

"Lovely darling," Eva says. Jill drops the blue dress and sags, and though Eva knows her response is not that which is required, it is hard to think what would be enough. Jill marches away once more, and Eva reaches for a guilty pleasure. She picks the small cigar from where she left it on an oversized ashtray and uses her new 'Cuba' lighter to gently puff. The effect creates an aroma without much inhalation, and Eva marvels at the audacity of smoking in a hotel room. How much longer, she wonders.

Through the tendrils of smoke she continues her study of the building opposite. What looks like a small tree has grown through a balcony, wound its way through some intricate ironwork, twisted up a small column, and triumphantly flowered, unaware it is exposing its roots below the balcony for all to see.

"I'd feel better if I could take off some weight, but it doesn't seem to want to shift." Jill's voice washes over her as Eva looks back down to street level. A small bright yellow tin can of a Lada, circa 1990, weaves round the green and pink car conversationalists, and a bicycle rickshaw follows the Lada through the tiny gap. Easy. The rickshaw driver looks up rather than in the direction he is driving and Eva follows his gaze. An elongated black bird lands on an ageing telephone cable causing it to bounce from post to post, like some game, whilst his other avian compatriots sit preening themselves in loops of cables, which mimic the flaccid stems of the banyan trees. Do those cables ever snap? Does it matter in a country where everything gets fixed somehow?

Suddenly Eva doesn't want to take their flight tomorrow, back to the same old. She needed a new boiler, then to replace her vacuum cleaner, and go online because everybody had to update their 'energy plans', and what about her lapsed contents insurance, and the daily pilgrimage to the supermarket. Her letter box was full of the screams of hysterical consumerism; 'save 40% on new pvc glazing', 'Pizza deliveries free within 2 miles', 'Two months free on your Annual Health Plan?' Being older didn't seem to allow you to dodge the sheer confused mess of it all. On a recent car trip, her three-year-old granddaughter had excitedly pointed out the letter 'M' from a foodchain, learning the alphabet apparently already entwined with brands. But here it didn't exist and she'd enjoyed eight whole days of no billboards, no leaflets, no cold calls, no advertising. Heaven.

Eva inhales, then allows the captured tendrils their escape. They billow and dissipate at the window, where glass silences what Eva knows of the cacophonic accompaniment to the scene. The hum of traffic, horns, and inescapable music.

"Damn, the deodorants run out. I'll smell like a horse," Jill shouts.

Yes, the smell of Havana is redolent of the disreputable and alluring odour of diesel fumes and cigar smoke.

"Marvellous," Eva says.

"Sorry?" Jill walks up to Eva, then follows her gaze out, looking around for what's 'marvellous'. After a few moments she gives up, and turns away.

"There's nothing good about aging is there?" Jill's cracked voice demands a response. Eva feels pulled, unwilling to get into this conversation leading nowhere. Perhaps if she were back in her little flat in Blackheath, with rain drumming the window and her arthritis playing up, and Jill sitting there pouring the tea, then they could both follow the same old grooves, but here?

She must fill the pause between them, but lets it sit. Instead, another gentle puff of cigar, and enjoyment of the obfuscated scene. She looks to the left, away from Jill and down to where the street ends. Like a missing tooth, the street end bears no building. Instead there is a simple landscaped square of short dusty palms, marking where one has fallen and not been replaced. Ultimately, as Eva has heard it described, searing heat and bitter cold break through the concrete flesh of a building, allowing water to worm its way to the hidden steel supports within. Once its bones have been rusted, then the steel swells and bursts apart corporeal concrete, in such a way that when enough damage has accrued the whole building, sagging and bowing, has been known to simply collapse.

Not everything can simply be repaired again and again, apparently.

Eva carefully stubs out the cigar, a taste to be savoured in small quantities. She stands, walks a few paces and puts her hand to the glass. Of course she is separated from the reality of Havana. In the street below, the peppermint Buick and the pink Cadillac have finished their pow wow, arms wave and they pull away. She could buy that ride for a bunch of dollars. Maybe she would stand up in the open top, force Jill to stand too and risk the breeze upsetting her hair. But it was all pretence. They'd both traded passion in for comfort far too many years ago to mention now. The salsa was for watching only.

"I'm ready," Jill says from behind her, and Eva reluctantly turns away from the decorous vista of decay. Unselfconscious, Havana has thrown on her most colourful clothes, wears her age with pride, and accepts her decline. Could it be that easy?

Jill stands as straight as a soldier on parade, ready to descend to a foyer commandeered half a century ago by Fidel's revolutionaries. On the dressing table behind her, sit the latest face cream and the best branded hair straighteners, whilst a strappy leather handbag over her arm is a riot of looped designer logo in gold.

She turns her brittle smile of preserved beauty up a notch, the signal to go.

The last night out then.

They wait a long time before the antiquated lift deposits them into the foyer of concreted stateliness, then the short stroll through its glass doors to the sweaty, clamouring city beyond. At her back now, the glorious block of Havana Libre Hotel, icon of the '50s, plots its capitalist revival. Because even if she could stay, that didn't mean Havana would remain unchanged.

All it had taken was one very old man to die and her Havana begins to change. She was an old fool. Clinging to the present, crumbling into the future.

She's back. I catch her eyes in my headlights

and snatch a glimpse as she darts across the road and behind a parked car, before being consumed by shadow. Was that really a sandwich in her mouth still wrapped in cellophane? A neighbour's gift most probably. Though I like to imagine it was gained in some high risk escapade, where she wriggled out of a fix by the skin of her sharp white teeth. Smart that's what she is. But how smart? It reminds me of that joke. A man is in the cinema and sees a fox sitting in the seat beside him. "Are you a fox?" he asks. "Yes" she replies. "What're you doing watching this film?" He says. The fox replies "well, I liked the book."

ROUNDABOUT

David watched the waitress, cloth and spray in hand, turn from the adjacent table, hesitate then walk away. He tipped his empty latte glass and ran the spoon in a slow circle around the last of the froth. Today was a day he could take as much time as he wanted. He could do what the hell he wanted, when he wanted, and there was nothing *she*, the vixen, could do about it.

He shivered, feeling the cold through the window. So. Where next? Charlie had made it clear that three months was enough sofa-squatting, and 'joked' that he was probably itching to move on. Yeah right. Code. His best friend had morphed from the Lord of Misrule, to an uptight prick with his own set of rules and regulations—the tea goes here, put the toothpaste there, turn the lamps off at night, pick your clothes up and the bedding goes there, and so on. Didn't anybody get that finishing a fifteen-year relationship, one you'd been in since you were seventeen for God's sake, took time to come back from? He'd had to leave the flat of course, and then bam, the redundancy came. Still. That's what he'd wanted for so long, wasn't it? Freedom? The whiskey,

105

full ashtrays, late night rants, and private tears were paving his way to—somewhere. He'd play the Xbox, be the big kahuna, and snap out of it soon, wouldn't he?

He couldn't stay missing Suzie forever, could he?

He wiped a circle in the misted window and a motorist waiting for the green stared right back at him. The car sported a frosted top, the wing mirrors crisped-out in white, and emissions fluffed into white clouds. The traffic had backed up and wasn't going anywhere, even the cyclists were impeded by the jam.

Waiting then.

He looked away, to where a woman stood at the intersection wrapped in a coat like a duvet. He could just see an edge of blonde hair peeping from her hood, and willed her to turn, only when she did he saw her face was quite lined and plain. He hadn't seen Suze in three whole months, but blonde hair still had him snap to attention, hoping what? It was her? Maybe she'd cut that sheen of long hair anyway, out of spite, though he couldn't imagine her any other way, inconceivable she could change without him. Maybe that had been the problem. She'd finish his sentences, he'd butt into her jokes, and even their bodies knew too well the same old map to follow. The journey from fresh, exciting love-making, to dull, predictable, tired sex. How many types of unsatisfactory sex can there be?

She never did become pregnant again, not after that miscarriage at seventeen. He fumbled for an indigestion tablet in his pocket, feeling the familiar tightness in his chest. It often helped if he thought of something, anything else, and willed himself to simply grasp any number of fun things he'd been disallowed from doing on account of shacking up too young. Perhaps he'd go to the *Dog and Bell* for a bit, he needed to forget, to mash his memory up a bit. You always felt better the next day, kind of purged and clear.

"Can I take this?" Without waiting for his response a man swivelled David's spare chair from his table. The café had filled up with the lunchtime crowd and the growing queue squeezed up to the door. He got up, checked his pockets for his packet of Marlboros and Charlie's key, then shifted his padded parka on. A cigarette, then go back to Charlie's for some thinking time. Caught in the confusion of nowhere, he didn't clock the slim figure across the road immediately.

But when the blonde hair is flicked back, his attention is caught. A buzz of adrenaline kicks him in the sternum as he feels the thrill of recognition. It's Suze. Across the road, walking away from him, dressed in a trench coat with the collar up. But it is the familiarity of that rapid, clipped walk. It's her.

He pushed between the tables and earnt a look from the guy with his chair, then squeezed through the door against the queue. Eyes turned but he didn't care, because he didn't want to lose her. By the time he'd got outside, the traffic was on the move again. He thrust out his arm at the oncoming cars and crossed anyway to the accompaniment of horns. He caught a flick of coat as she turned left into Congress Street. He skipped into a half run and felt the frost-edged cuts to his lungs. A conspiracy of commuters headed directly towards him but he didn't deviate and they parted before him. His padded parka billowed out like pointed wings and he took his space, challenging those wrapped and insulated individuals to acknowledge him. He nudged the arm of a woman and her eyes slid from him as she clutched her handbag.

Over the top of the crowd, he saw the sheen of her blonde hair against her black coat and relaxed because he'd gained on her. Towering a head above everybody else, he pulled back his speed and matched her pace easily in his size tens. He'd given the flat up for her, but when he'd tried her landline a month ago, late at night, it was disconnected. He suspected she'd moved, and the thought infuriated him. He found himself running events through his mind, wondering if she'd handed him a loaded gun, got him to finish the relationship, but wanted out. It happened. But it was inconceivable that she would change, walk away from him, out of his life? He was still trying to grasp it, the elusive explanation for their split up. Perhaps the squabbles and irritations of everyday life—toothpaste lids, overtime, washing up, her job and his lack of, his friends and her friends, all the mundanities and life maintenance stuff heaped up in all their particularities. In other words, the sum of the small stuff.

He watched her retreating figure flicker in and out of the crowds, and tried to see it, grasp the incomprehension of it. He would stop her, shake her, hold her to account, demand she deny it wasn't real, because things would be different from now on. If he could only hold her again, he would be able to get through, make her understand him. He glimpsed a tease of her slim waist caught in the belt's cinch, the sway in her hips, and simply knew how easy it was to hold that hair like a coil in one hand. How it had felt to kiss her neck. Did he? Was that memory real? He weighed catching up to her against the intoxication of his current tracking, and decided to play it out. More rope to hang herself with? He'd know soon enough.

She slowed down as if she was about to cross the road, so he edged left as she turned, checked the road was clear, then stepped out and over. He watched as she pulled out her phone and checked something. What? Was it his imagination or did she look nervous, scared perhaps? They were two miles from her office in Tottenham Court Road, and three stops from their old flat. Had she tracked him down to Charlie's? Or was she lost?

Or on her way to meet another man? She wouldn't dare do such a thing to him, he would—he would. He shoved his hands into his wide pockets and sped up ever so slightly. She didn't know what he was capable of.

Does the man live here? Multi-million pound Georgian houses with pillars and wide marble steps to their right, and discreet brass plates of occasional select businesses. Perhaps she was seeing a solicitor, or—a private doctor? Was she ill? He needed to know, like he always did, everything about her, in the same way she'd always known everything about him. He hesitated, weighing the frustration of unanswered questions against the pleasing deception of shadowing her. He watched her walk past the houses, skirting a private park to their left, ringed in mist and secrecy, and merely followed. He passed a power of parked cars—Range Rovers, Mercedes, and Audis, and fingered Charlie's keys in his pocket, imagined with a click of the fob, a Mercedes' lights would flash him a greeting. Or that he could patter up those marble steps and insert the key, opening wide the dove grey door to reveal the luxurious interior. The ambiguity of the mist smudged out connecting points, the between spaces, rendering anything possible. He imagined, with every billowing breath out, he was divested of himself; and with every breath in, he drank up the affluence of the street. He walked a little taller, held out his arm, and pointed to her back. Surely his desire, his power, was strong enough that any moment she would find herself turning back to him.

He blinked and she disappeared.

Superman deflated, he hurried to catch up with his Lois Lane, then slowed when he saw the opening into the alley. He hung back. No room for cars here, just the tall sides of the buildings rendered in frost and a straight rimmed pavement. He counted his frigid breath billow five times, then followed. Light was snatched away and he pulled the sides of his coat together. Was there enough privacy here, he wondered, that he could catch up to her? Press his hand to her mouth, dig his fingers in her arm and frogmarch her, then shove her hard up against the wall, push into her, so her coat was smeared against the dank wall, thumb her lipstick across her face, lick her cheek, take a handful of that precious hair and— Bam. Smack her stupid head back. Because who did she think she was except his. His to do whatever he wanted with. Oh the smiles would come back then surely. That was his mistake, not containing her in the right spaces. This place would do, to ensure she knew what she was. That last time they'd made love, when he'd been tight up against her and felt her resistance to him, the lips that endured kisses, her withheld pleasure. In this tight space nothing could be withheld. His steps, faster now, a staccato beat, amplified. He could—have it—they said. Now. Have. Dark. Tight. Cold. Hard.

Silhouetted in a sharp oblong of light at the end of the dark alley, he saw her look both ways and hesitate, her hands in her pockets. Butterfly lightness snapped her existence out and she was gone.

He ran to the end of the alley, rounded the corner and was nailed by bright lights. Street market stalls, humbug striped, dusted in fairy lights. His view was obscured by a man grasping a cut Christmas tree

111

and banging it down hard, fluffing its branches. He ignored its heady smell and snatched looks in all directions hampered by people who shuffled around the festive obstacles. They stopped. They snatched conversations and impeded his progress. A profusion of piled oranges, clementines, and satsumas blocked his way. He turned and Xmas jumpers twisted in the air, suspended, tinsel colours smacked the senses whilst all the time there was the 'ho ho ho' of a giant Santa who bobbed and swayed.

The sun came out and he was dazzled. Nothing it did not see. Dear God, was he really doing this? Stalking her? He turned and looked back into the dark alley. Where had all those disgusting thoughts come from? He imagined them dripping down the sides of the dank walls. Would he really have done anything? Christ, who was he? He stood, a passive bystander, brushed by strangers nudged this way and that. A little girl looked up at him as if he were the tallest tree in the forest before her granny pulled her away. A bloke with no anchor points, that's what he was. Lost. He looked down and a baby stared widely back at him, snugged tightly into its buggy as mum selected socks. Would they have got there, eventually, after the tragedy of the miscarriage? Could they have got that far and had a 'family'? He thinks, no, *knows* he would have liked it.

Every last Sunday of the month, they'd visited her mum and dad in Brighton. Her mother still baked cakes, and made conversation, her father would guide him around the garden, explain the trouble with the pond lining, and point out damselfly larvae. He had a garage and a shed, and David could almost, *almost* grasp it. Sweet, that's what they'd been. No wonder Suzie smiled so much and expected the best. He held his face up then, felt the weak sunshine behind his closed eyes. Saw that blonde hair glow once more. God what a mean bastard he'd been. Just taking it all. Of course she loved him, and okay, yes he loved her. If only. He opened his eyes to the incessant assemblage of people on the move, walking, talking, laughing, and *belonging* to somebody.

He was lost without her.

Only there she was. His 'if only' held something at a stall, examined it, then handed over money and put it into her handbag. Without a backward glance, she turned and walked purposefully through the crowds away from him.

He followed her. This time, pulled, not driven, wanting to hold that thing again. Do whatever it took to have it back. He stepped into and through the confusion of crowd, losing her often, feeling smaller, more obscure. More careful too, not to barge past those around him, who were now part of that thing he desired. The rhythm of his steps, irregular, as he changed micro direction, moving with the crowd, not pushing. And the rhythm said: Confess. Apologise. Grasp. Confusion. *Sorry, but you are in my thoughts all the time, I even think like you now. You are in me always, because we grew together.* Just see me. And I will. Exist again. Help me see.

113

The market stalls became more spaced out, the crowd thinned, as he followed her down a twisting pedestrianised road. The mist grew thicker. Should he run up to her now indistinct form, or wait until she found her destination? Then what?

He walked on. It was not that he resolved to wait, more that he was confused into inaction, left blankly following. The sun resigned its brilliance to the vague domination of the mist, and his thoughts followed, overlapping, abstruse, his only anchor the muffled sound of her steps. Wait. Wait. Wait. Wait. His step loud, hers the faintest of echoes, but the rhythm lulled him, turned him into a follower. The road straightened and morphed into those typical of many in London, the blitz having picked out holes in the Victorian terraces, leaving a hotch potch of architecture styles. The mist rounded their edges, detached them one from the other, and it felt like a presentation laid out on his behalf. Perhaps 'they', Suze and him, could have lived there in the terrace. Or what about the maisonette with the bay windows? So that could have been their Citroen, with a domed frosted top, and smiling headlight eyes. She would have liked that garden there, all pebbled with a lavender centre. What would have been his choices, his opinions and preferences?

Wait. Wait. Wait. Wait. Who was he exactly without her? How long had he been walking for? What was he doing?

He was losing her, that's what was happening.

114

No, wait. Wait. Wait. He didn't want to face that. But it felt like it came at him.

Something approached him.

He snapped his head, this way and that, scanned the unreadable mist. Surrounded by all those supposed choices, panic changed the rhythm of his steps.

Wait. Run. No. Stop. What? Wait. Where is she? He didn't feel himself. Something came and he couldn't stop it. He was porous. A nothing. He was an idea of himself.

A bird flashed past him then soared up, calling 'haaa haaa haaa' before disappearing. He hugged himself and searched the greyness, aching for detail. Somewhere up there, silver against grey, it wheeled wide circles, dissected the hunter and the hunted, the lover and the loved. Laughed at the joke. It held his story in its crystal eye and it seemed to him that perhaps it wasn't possible to extract himself from her. He had never been himself. Distant. Disconnected. Dear God, what was he doing? He was losing it.

Mist roiled and he stopped, chest heaving. It hit. He let go then. Let it come at him on wings. Great lugs of sobs shook him. He missed her so badly. Claws in his chest.

I am not myself.

It won't let go.

115

I can't let it go.

I am lost.

Grief, universal and impersonal. It took its inarticulate time. It worked him over.

How long have I been here? I wipe my eyes and face with my hands, unable to distinguish between tears and wet mist, and although I'm still in pain, at least I'm feeling something. Around me the fog is even thicker, all detail rendered unnecessary, and it's true, particularities don't matter anymore, because who am I without us? I am more myself now I know nothing. Somebody has taken my skin off, and the mist is in me. I am a wet, raw piece of meat.

I stumble forward into thick mist, terrified because I can't hear the footsteps anymore. I put my arms out like I'm blind, and it's so thick I can't even see my shoes. My breath comes in thick bubbling sobs. I'm staring so hard, I'm not blinking, just willing myself to see a flash of hair, or coat. I don't know how long I stumble like that for, but finally I think I see a yellowed glow. The form seems more distant, the footsteps hardly discernible, indistinct luminosity the clearest feature. I'm not sure how far I've walked or where we are, but I can't lose it now.

We settle into a rhythm.

Have I given up?

When will I give up?

Another winter. A warm room. A tangle of limbs rendered rainbow bright by the Christmas lights. I play with a strand of hair, thumb the softness of cheek, and look into those eyes. I want to be behind them, thinking those thoughts, really understand what it is like to be that person. Be the loved and the lover in a perfect empathic circle. Trapped in our bodies, it is all we have, the inadequate tool of empathy. How is it to look through those eyes, to touch and feel? In that moment I feel so close and such a deep love. I soften, and the line between us blurs.

She lets me in. He lets me in.

I close my eyes and walk through the mist. Now there is no distinction between inside and outside, I am porous, and take in the cold. I am thinned out, roil and stir with the slightest of breezes. I am lost. I have lost. I hold my hand up in front of me and there is a shock of flesh, diamonds clinging to the fingertips. It is something to focus on, and I have to try and hold on. I slide my fingers down the length of my coat, the sensation of damp cloth secures me to myself, and I feel for and tighten my belt then pull my collar up higher. My steps are hesitant now. Shorter. And it is not long before I feel it. The hairs on my neck prickle in agreement, and the unsettling thought refuses to lie down.

I am being followed.

My breath comes short and tight, and for a while I can't force myself to turn and look back.

117

Perhaps if I pretend it is not there, then it won't be. Perhaps if I pretend a lot of things. Like let's pretend the relationship is not over. Let's pretend if I keep busy and move forwards, the past doesn't exist, and I don't have to see it. I fumble in my pocket and my fingers connect with the Christmas globe I bought earlier. I push it aside to grasp for my phone and pull it out, but there is still no signal, so no map appears, just an empty grey grid.

I must do this, I must face up to things and turn and confront whatever is there. Teeth gritted, jaw clenched, I turn.

There is nothing there.

No, wait.

Wings. Something with wide wings flapping.

I turn back and start running, I don't care. The sound of my steps is a sharp staccato, cutting through the mist, so I run faster. I just need to recognise something, anything. This thing will swallow me whole, and I won't be able to function, so I need the familiar. I'm not ready, not yet, and I don't want to feel the pain of it.

I turn another corner.

And sob with relief as a busy junction establishes itself. Cars sit, fogging up, chugging out plumes, impatient for the green. A woman in a thick coat like a duvet, with blonde hair, stands waiting for a cab. Across the road there is a shoe repair shop, and next to it a coffee shop. I stop for a moment and allow my breath to calm. I look again at my phone, and although there is still no map, I am reassured by the normality of it all. Enough to smile out loud. I smooth my hair down and tuck it into the inside of my trench coat. It won't stay there, but finds its way back out and down.

He used to love my blonde hair, play with strands of it. Kiss them even. I'd catch his large hand, enjoy its roughness and plant a kiss on the palm. I start to walk again, wanting to shake the thoughts out of me, because sometimes I feel I know him so well he is in me. If I can stop thinking about him then I can just get somewhere different. Is that what love is, knowing somebody so well you're in their skin? It's got so bad that I think I see him on every street corner.

Like now, across the road, sitting by the fogged up coffee shop window.

No, I can't think about him. I smile, because I'm aware people may be looking at me, and I want to seem in control. It's confusing you see, because I feel I've been here before. That's good, isn't it? The coffee shop looks warm and inviting, and I watch as a waitress, cloth and spray in hand, busies around, cleaning tables. Perhaps I should go in? I hesitate.

My breath billows, like curling dragon smoke it loops round. Like—

Circles.

I know I should 'move on' as they say, but I can't seem to do it, I can't face the awful—awful—I've just got to keep moving and it can't get me. I dig my heels in and walk a little faster. No, he wanted time didn't he?

Just a little more time he'd said.

So sometimes you feel like you're going in circles. You need to escape the city. But there's a problem. You sit on the edge of your wooden boat, dig your foot into the river's gravel and try to work it out. Never mind the suitcase. How do you get the fox, chicken and corn across to the other side? All the while a pair of bright orange eyes bore into you. She's a wise old fox this one, yet with such a sweet pointy face, and a black button nose, and you swear she's smiling at you, because you can see those white incisors each side. After a while, you can't bear her gaze anymore and ask her, 'okay, okay, what would you do?' 'Well' she says, 'I will help you do this in one trip. I will kindly transport the chicken and corn for you.' 'You will?' I ask, 'how?' 'In my belly', she responds sweetly.

STREETS AHEAD

She would have to upgrade. Just another one of those life maintenance tasks everybody engaged in, like switching and swopping. Amy leant back from her computer and rolled the stiff grind of knots around her shoulders. She wouldn't have felt this tired if it hadn't taken two hours to swop their electricity supply.

Downstairs, the fridge door slammed and the snap of a ring pull signalled Adrian's return from the gym. She straightened and clattered in the specs for the next phone model up, pressed enter, and a bewildering array of ads and comparison websites snapped up. Should she get a contract or buy outright? Maybe a contract didn't feel so painful. Another click, and a bewildering selection of colours, models, memory capacities, networks, and prices appeared. Slowly she went through clicking the left hand choices, based on her current phone, which was light and easy and such a shame it was out of date. She hovered the cursor over the enter button and carefully reviewed her choice of ticks. Next would come 'Sort by price, low to high'.

"No, you want a younger model." Adrian leant over her. His arm brushed her face as he checked the screen. He smelt all fresh and lemony, from the gym soap no doubt, and she breathed in his presence. His hand covered hers on the mouse as he clicked and cleared her choices.

"There. That's what you want." He smiled at the screen, stretched up, and walked out.

"Thank you," Amy called, then stared at a website featuring the newest 'buy outright' models. Lord, the prices.

"Early night for me," he called back, and she heard him walk into the bedroom. Oh. She gave it a few moments, then clicked the cross, and watched the bewildering array of phones snap into oblivion. She'd get it done tomorrow, Saturday.

Twenty minutes later, freshly showered, she came into the dark bedroom and slid into the bed beside him. His body was turned away, so she spooned him, enjoying his solidness, the feel of his sides, and waited for him to register the contact. Nothing. She buried her face in the curve of his neck and fell asleep to the smell of their mismatched soaps.

Amy woke the next morning, turned over, and registered the empty hollow beside her. An indistinct radio burble drifted up the stairs, as did a waft of fresh coffee. She grabbed the clock, and a wave of embarrassment wrapped itself around her as securely as the twisted duvet, when it displayed

9.05am. What a lazy bones she was. In the hallway, she snatched Friday's mail from the table and wandered into the kitchen. Adrian stood with his back to her, holding a spatula in one hand and texting with the other. Oh my, he loved his phone.

She reached to hug him from behind, and he jumped.

"Amy, don't. The phone nearly ended up in the frying pan." He tucked the phone into the pocket of his jeans and adjusted his stance, all his attention now on the large frying pan, and the eggs and bacon and tomatoes. For a moment, she considered wrapping her arms around the wall of his back, but settled on a stroke down his spine, before she turned and sat at the breakfast bar and opened the first of the letters. '*We've got it covered*', read the strap line and her heart sank. The emergency breakdown cover renewal for their Citroen. The next line read '*You don't need to do a thing*', so she instantly scanned the letter, and there in small print was £165. Right, so if she didn't 'do a thing', they'd put their hand into her bank account. Okay, but she'd deal with that after the upgrade. The next envelope announced '*Peace of Mind*' and featured a picture of a happy young professional with their arms splayed wide, and an expanse of blue sky, which took up the top half of the letter. '*Home insurance. We beat any quote.*' She'd have to check when theirs was next up for renewal? After she'd taken the electricity reading, because she'd swopped last night, and they'd need it.

Adrian slapped the breakfast plate down on the post in front of her and took a seat.

"Thank you, sweetheart." He was simply too good for her, and she would have kissed him on the cheek, except he had started shovelling egg, showing off his strong jawline to good effect. He took a slurp of coffee and she looked around for her cup. He must have been up sometime, because he'd made coffee for one.

"Fancy the market today?" she said.

He stopped mid-munch, then wiped some egg from his mouth.

"Babes, I've got to go into work."

So they gave him a promotion, but what was he, a slave they could call on to work all hours?

"It's relentless." He said.

"Poor you," she said.

"Would you mind doing the washing run? I would, only…."

"Sure."

He started shovelling in breakfast quicker, and she rubbed his arm. The poor guy hardly got a life.

"Onwards and upwards," he said, wiped his lips, sprung up, and she hardly had time to swivel the

126

stool round before a kiss landed on the top of her head.

"You don't mind doing the food shop do you?" he shouted back at her.

"Okay."

"Oh, don't forget my cousin Sophie's leaving present?" He turned and smiled lopsidedly. She took in all of him. The Paul Smith shirt and how good he always looked in CK jeans, as he searched the pockets for the car keys and checked his mobile.

"Sure. What time will you be back?"

"And treat yourself. Get that upgrade."

The front door slammed and Amy turned back to survey the kitchen. She raised her hand to shield her eyes as the spring sun spot lit the grubby kitchen surface, strewn with eggs shells, empty packets, cups, plates, squeezed out tea bags, and three used pans. Beyond which, her attention was directed to their grimy wood floor and dust on the dresser. OK, kitchen first then. Surfaces. Then floor. Dishwasher. Then bins. Hoover. Dust. Then car Insurance ring around. Then electricity reading. Home Insurance. Then strip bedding. Washing run. Then food shop, and Sophie's present. Then—upgrade.

By 3pm, she found herself plodding around the supermarket with the word upgrade thumping in her aching head. By 4pm, seated at the computer once more, a strange thing happened. All her usual reserve and cautiousness was released in one heady act of spending. She found herself clicking 'Ready to Collect' on the top range silver/white model, five-star reviews, plenty of storage, and superior camera. In fact, if she could get to the shop before 5pm, she could pick it up, *and* meet Adrian from work. Wow. Upgraded. Wouldn't Adrian be pleased?

Only he'd taken their car, so she'd have to forgo make-up and run like crazy to make it for 5pm. She shut the door, then belted her long coat securely, so her baggy leggings didn't show. She tried her best to smooth her unbrushed hair, hoping her roots weren't showing, and wishing the sun came with a 'brilliance' control button, because it made her head throb. When the 47 bus appeared, she chased it down, then sweaty and panting, relented and loosened the long coat. She picked at the bobbles on her ageing grey jumper, and checked she had her ID in her purse. They could be fussy about these things with expensive upgrades.

There was no problem. Nursing the upgrade in its gold and white packaging, she paused to cross at the corner of Mortimer Street and Gloucester Circus.

And there was her Citroen.

Yet Adrian worked half a mile down Mortimer and up the High Street. She turned, drawn towards it, past the Georgian houses, past the man in the crisp blue suit and tie whose black patent shoes clip clopped, past the eyes that flickered towards her sweating face, raking over the tatty jumper and baggy leggings. She slowed down, wondering whether to turn back. The sound of laughter issued from behind a black Range Rover, and she caught sight of two heads, one blond, the other dark. The couple exchanged a kiss. It was only when they broke away that Amy saw him.

Was that...?

His back was towards her, but she watched the young woman flip back her long blond hair and adjust her designer shades higher. Impressions of a cream blouse, lilac pencil skirt encasing long, long legs, finished off by matching cream kitten heels. A cool and astonishing beauty. Whose angled fatless hips were now being displayed and on show by the man's hands which casually held them. The couple curled into each other like they had been designed that way.

"Adrian?"

He turned, and at first looked over and around her, then back again, and focused.

Silence.

Honey Blonde examined her too, then raised an arched eyebrow at Adrian. She should say something.

"I've upgraded." She held the phone out. Honey Blonde's smile faded. She moved away slightly but one of his hands remained on her hip.

"It's a silver and white finish."

Honey Blonde's expression hardened and she backed away further.

"Adrian?"

He looked at her fully then, took her all in, and she saw herself through his eyes.

A toss of mane, and Honey Blonde stalked away. Adrian hesitated.

"Adrian?"

He turned one way, then the other, staring at Honey Blonde's retreating back, before casting a furious glance at her. Why would he be angry with me? If this was what she thought it was, then he would apologise about an aberrant impulse? Some mistake?

"Yes. I heard you," he said.

And headed after the Blonde.

"Adrian?"

The phone dropped from her hand, as he stretched the distance between them to catch up with Honey Blonde. She couldn't see much because of her tears then, but she heard perfectly well as his shout rang back.

Upgraded.

It happens so fast, there is no time to apply foot to break. A flicker of movement in my right eye is followed by the smack of an impact to the bonnet. A soft thwump sound follows, of something soft travelling under the car.

I want to pretend it hasn't happened. Lose myself in make believe. I sit in a warm bubble of car, perfectly safe and well, yet there's something else here with me now. A pain that chews away behind my breast bone.

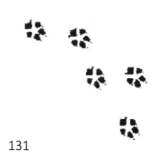

IN AND AROUND THE PHARMACY

Pain was nesting. She liked to nest, but it was only possible when she became many. She—they—had been here before and it was a good place. It helped—it made the slipping in, the settling much easier. She twisted and rooted down hard against the vertebrae and multiplied. Now she was more, she could travel in all directions, diving, flicking and swimming in synovial fluid, sparking from nerve to nerve, racing its length, sighing along the spine meninges, then greeting her sisters as they arrived at the brain. Mostly Pain travelled, so it felt good to nest. So much better than feeling stretched. When she'd have to jump the distance from nerve to nerve, transparent, hardly in existence, searching, until she found somewhere. Then Pain liked to root hard up against tissue, cartilage and bone and become many. When she was nesting she—they— could hum, a throbbing rhythm. She would oscillate with her sisters, rippling, pulsating through fluid, blood, bone and sinew. The throb would mount, a fine orchestration of sharpness and roundness. If Pain could think, she would express it as a fine musical pleasure. Yes. It was good here.

It seemed to Sandra there was very little discernment about the man's choices. He simply grabbed three random tubes off the shelf and shuffled slowly to her counter and pushed Backease, Roltavol, and Sherringham's Back Rub at her. He then stared straight past her to the shelves beyond the painkillers selection.

"I'll have the Solpa-Plus Extra 24 tablets. And I'll take the Nurofen Extra, tablet form please. Thanks."

"Have you taken these before?" she said.

"Yes, yes."

Sandra felt herself bristle at his irritability. He probably thought she was a sales assistant like all the others did and not a fully trained and experienced pharmacist. She pulled herself up onto her heels, familiar with the annoyance of being only five foot two. He had not looked at her once, just fumbled in his wallet for a note. He was just a large middle aged man puffed up with impatience, but it still rankled. It wasn't that he was fat, just large in quite a gristly way. She would be polite, of course, but he had to understand.

"You know you mustn't take the creams with the tablets, don't you? These contain painkillers as well."

He stared at her. Finally he saw her.

"Yes, yes."

134

Sandra bagged his items briskly and took the proffered card. He leaned forwards and she noticed his hands, like large paws resting his weight on the counter and inadvertently crushing the edges of the stacked packets of cough sweets. Transaction complete, Sandra watched as the man turned, ripped apart the soft plastic bag and opened the packet of painkillers. The folded square of contraindications advice fell to the floor. A young mother with a buggy hovered behind him, expecting him to move away from the queue, edging the buggy's wheels to within inches of him. The man seemed oblivious to his own large presence, and instead rested his weight backwards once more on the long-suffering lozenge section. He popped the pills out of their foil backs and the woman was forced to wait. Sandra was sure she counted three, not two tablets, as he threw them into the back of his mouth and tipped his head jerkily in an effort to swallow without water. Finally, the pressure on her afflicted lozenges was released and he moved away, lumbered towards the door.

Another piece of awkward theatre was enacted as the man pulled on the door, fought weakly with its tension, and performed a strange sideways dance to extricate himself from the shop. In pain then. A familiar feeling nagged at her, but she tried not to give it room. Of course she found him repulsive. All of them repulsed her. The old people, with their creeping sicknesses, the screaming children with hacking coughs, the 'confiders', hypochondriacs, lingering over the minutiae of symptoms. What the disorder felt like, their physical frailties, and what was wrong with them. Always, always, what was wrong with them? As if she cared. As if they thought she did this for pleasure. Tended their pains with pleasure. But these were dangerous thoughts not to be dwelt on. These were their concerns, not hers. Briskly, Sandra busied herself with the next transaction, and the shadow thoughts passed.

If Pain had ears, she would say it sounded like thick, fat snow falling. Something muffled and enveloped them. They slowed down. Moving was harder too and it was difficult to greet each other. But Pain was stubborn. She would not move. She'd sit and wait it out. She hummed a little and mused. She knew he didn't want her to go. He'd invited her and there was no need to leave. He needed her. It was hard though and Pain felt fearful. It was always this loss of self she feared. Didn't he know, she was part of him? Maybe she would sleep for a bit. She and her sisters would acquiesce, lie down, there was time. She could be patient.

Anne wrapped her dressing gown around her tightly and padded down the stairs. What was the silly bugger doing now? Didn't he know he was keeping her awake? Didn't he know she could hear him pace around, or the snick of the kitchen cupboard doors open and close from all the way upstairs? Where was he anyway? She wandered from the empty kitchen to the front room where lamplight radiated from beneath the closed door.

"What the bloody hell are you doing?" she said.

"What the bloody hell do you think I am doing?" he answered.

The silly bugger lay flat on the floor with his knees bent. His silhouette against the half-light reminded Anne of a pregnant woman doing some sort of Pilates exercise, except he wasn't pregnant, just 'beefy'. That's what he called it.

"Go back to sleep woman."

Nice. Sure. It took her an age to get to sleep these days and now wide awake it would take her hours to get back to sleep. How dare he do this to her. He could be so selfish sometimes.

"I don't know why you don't go to the doctor's," she said.

"Because the ruddy doctors can't do anything for..."

"You don't know that," she said.

"Yes, I do!"

And now he shouted at her. Well.

"How dare you shout? Anyone would think it was my fault you've got a bit of backache."

In the dim light, his eyes glittered at her and for a moment he looked murderous. Trickery. Just the light. What did he have to be angry at? A lot less than she did. A life of tediousness had been her lot when she took up with Mr Cautious there. With his constant worrying about money all the time and all the time moaning about his bloody job. As if she wanted to listen to that all day. As if she wanted to stare at his profile every night, up-lit by the glow from the TV, constantly chattering out his choice of snooker and golf events. It had been his choice of a life. Tedious. The man was tedious. He could have it back. Every ounce of bloody anger.

"I don't have to take this," she said.

"Give over."

"Sort yourself out."

"I'm in pain!" he said.

He raised himself a couple of inches and gritted his teeth in fury. In the mirror above the fireplace she caught sight of herself, her tired, doughy face and the shock of her greying dishevelled hair. If he had loved her she would not look like this. The loved are never made ugly this way. Disappointment pinched her mouth, turning the corners down, anger etched her lines deep. All his doing. The orange satin lampshade dangled with bobbles behind his head and lent him a foolish element like he wore a comic fez. She sighed, unable to keep it up.

"Take another painkiller. Go down to Dr Anthony's tomorrow morning."

She left him lying there in his striped M&S pyjamas. The bottom two buttons of his top were busted and gave space to his spreading belly fat. She hugged her dressing gown around her as if cold, then brushed the familiar towelling with her fingers and mounted back up the stairs. She felt bruised around the heart, a familiar feeling. Pain. Was it real pain? Was there something wrong with her heart and she just didn't know it? It felt real. Nonsense, how could feelings hurt you, they didn't exist in any physical sense. She just needed a good night's sleep, that's all. She sat on the bed then twisted back into the same warm hollow from earlier and pulled the duvet up. Her mind kept throwing up that last picture of his vicious glare. They'd shared twenty-five years of married life and that counted for something didn't it? The good and the... bad. Like Calum. On 27th August each year they'd go together to visit Calum in Hither Green Cemetery. 'Calum Baker. Fell asleep, aged one day'. Their angel. What with all that history, well, you made your bed and you had to bloody well lie in it didn't you. She thought perhaps he might hate her. Well, she hated him too at times. There was the size of it. She turned onto her good side and wedged the pillow to the right height. Still, she mused. At least they had each other.

Pain twisted and danced, tumbled and dived. The numbness was gone now, and there was more fluid to move easefully within. Pain and her sisters coursed through the host, jumping the gaps, delighted at the responsive receptors that greeted them easily on arrival in the brain. The host was providing all sorts of good things to feast upon now and she would grow further. What made this host feel so good was the fight. It was a healthy host and pain felt comfortable and sustained. Soon she and her sister's hum would fill their new home and spread, creating a song. Pain felt she was at reaching her fullest potential.

Judging by the man's inclination forwards, as he walked painfully towards her, Eleanor guessed it would be a classic inflammation around the L4 or L5 vertebrae, maybe with sacral iliac joint pain. She'd ask if it ran down the leg too and caused him sciatic pain. Chair acupressure was really best for upper back, shoulders and neck so it would be awkward for her bending that low.

"Are you free now?"

"Yes, how long would you like?" Eleanor said, wiping the acupressure chair down with a wet wipe,~~and~~ assessing the man's height. She loosened the lever close to the headrest and pulled it up a couple of inches before re-setting it.

"Forty-five minutes?"

Good. At least the man hadn't asked for twenty minutes and a miracle cure, though forty-five minutes wasn't exactly substantial. It amazed her how many clients would come in with chronic pain and inflammation, ask for ten minutes and expect the problem to disappear instantly. They would point to the bit that hurt repeatedly, like their body was a faulty machine, and ask her to work only on that part.

Sometimes when she relieved additional tensions in the back, she'd feel them tense up, irritated that she was wasting time on a fixed bit. They exacerbated their pain with anger at their body part, exhorting her to go deep and 'as hard as you like' into the offending shoulder or neck. The body, it appeared, was merely some sort of flawed carrying vessel for the all-important mind.

The man mounted the chair awkwardly and sagged into the seat, and it seemed to Eleanor that he wouldn't be questioning her about anything. He held himself cautiously, as if all movement ached and was tender, yet every now and then would jump a little at a hurt that was twinging and sharp. Wretched and pitiable were the two words that sprang to mind. Perhaps the usual struggle to give this client the massage he needed rather than that which he thought he wanted, would be possible today. Eleanor started with some gentle presses down either side of the erector spinae. It would be easy to feel the necessity to 'get tough' with this body, as it felt impenetrable and difficult to reach, but she resisted the reaction. If she tried too hard, he would not let her in, unconsciously toughening further. No, she would start gently.

Pain had a memory. That's why it was easier to return to somewhere she had been before. She even had a memory of before she was she. She was happy and allowed herself to think lovingly of another time and another host. That time Pain had started cosily in a cluster of cells, spreading rapidly, until it seemed they truly inhabited all the spaces of the host. It was the strangest feeling as Pain felt she had shape, almost being. They had sung most beautifully. A joyful time.

Eleanor felt the man relaxing and changed her stroke to gentle 'warm up' circular motions, still along either side of the spine. She would not hurry.

Pain's reverie was interrupted. Her sisters, it appeared, were not happy. Something was wrong, they cried. As they jumped from nerve to nerve, there was not enough stickiness. They slipped and slithered their way to the brain, where they were no longer welcomed in the same way. We are not wanted, they cried. Pain was irritated, annoyed at being pulled from the memory of herself at a glorious moment. How had that story gone? But she must attend to now and see what was happening.

For the first time in over a week, Simon finally felt himself relax a little. He'd had to call in sick this morning and that had made him feel even worse. He couldn't bring himself to say backache again as his boss would have little sympathy with that one, so he'd said flu. At that point he'd felt more scared of his own state of mind than he had about his boss being annoyed with him. What was wrong with him, was he cracking up or something? As he'd held the sink that morning, tentatively leaning forwards to clean his teeth, the pain in his back excruciating, he'd burst into tears. The embarrassment was intense, and he felt fearful of what he himself might do. No, no, this had been the right decision. He needed to sort his back out once and for all. He felt guilty though, feeling the soothing sensation of the therapist's hands. Her hands...

Eleanor's hands lifted gently. She changed position now to stand in front of her bowed client. The stance allowed her to bear down on her client's shoulders, both hands massaging the top of his back and shoulders. One two, one two, the rhythm was soothing in its methodical application. She would not go to the site of the pain yet, there was plenty of tension in the rest of the back. She could take her time.

It was true. She and her sisters had to jump further between the nerve endings. Were the spaces getting wider, or were they getting smaller? Pain surged around, checking the gaps, agitated by the thought of loss. They had become a self here, this was their home. This reminded her of something. What was it? It was important she remember. Pain travelled fast to the brain. Surely the host knew he needed her?

Anne would say this was a waste of money, Simon thought. He imagined what she would say if she could see him all nice and relaxed having a massage from another woman. She would be scornful of the indulgence more than anything. After all, she never had massages, why should he? Besides he deserved to—he should be stronger—if only he'd— perhaps if...

Eleanor felt the man tense up, adopting that 'held' stance which characterised his body at the start of the massage....

Pain rallied. He needed her, she felt it. She coiled and twisted and jabbed, tearing along his spinal cord. The speed of her swirled the synovial fluid around her home rendering it hot and red.

Eleanor stroked the man's spine rhythmically with the flat of her hands. It was not a move she had been taught on her course five years ago, but one that a fellow therapist had treated her to, which she'd found delectably relaxing and had adapted.

What was it he was thinking about? Simon couldn't remember. Oh well, if it was important it would come back.

Pain felt herself falling. Each time they jumped the spaces between the nerves now, some of her ceased to exist. Pleasure rendered the sides of the nerves smooth and the brain receptors closed. They were diminishing. She needed to work, to think, to stop this happening... There was something she needed to remember...

With circular motions, and as if by chance, Eleanor finally came to massage the man's lower back. She had felt the bulge of inflammation around L3-4, and the tenderness of the sacral iliac joint on the right, so kept her thumbs wide beside the spine when she applied the acupressure points.

It was something to do with the last host. It was difficult to think now, but Pain had to remember. In terror, she realised she was losing herself. What was it? There had been the joy of inhabiting such a large space, how she had been almost corporeal. She and her sisters had sung loud and ruled that body, but the body had grown weak and could not hold out any longer. Yes, that's right, that's what happened...

Eleanor was pleased to see the man was very relaxed, perhaps even asleep. Crossing her forearms, she used large sweeping movements across his lower back, careful to keep wide of the spine.

Pain feared death. Death of the host meant her own loss of existence, but surely this was different, this host was strong. We are dying, we are dying, cried her sisters in terror. Pain suffered and tried to remember. With that other host she had grown so strong, they had orchestrated the most beautiful agonies. But it was damaged too much, and that body died, abruptly signalling the end of the most beautiful glory. Pain had remembered screeching, long and loud, when they had realised what had happened. And that's when they had to... when they had to...

She pictured the vertebrae in her mind, their angle and position beneath the skin. Her thumbs curled in closer and glided around the lower back, gently palpating and pushing away that build-up of fluid. She was inside the body now, whilst that ticking, precise part of her remained apart reviewing herself and her actions. Stated simply, you couldn't do this job unless you were really 'into' bodies. Love I guess you'd call it. She never said this out loud, as people would think loving a body was sexual whereas this was more like deep appreciation of the wonder that was flesh. What was the mind without the body? The brain was a blind organ reliant on the senses to bring it to life. Less of 'I think, therefore I am', and more 'I feel, therefore I am'. We are our bodies.

Simon felt all smoothed out. Perhaps things were okay, it was all okay. This was good and he felt kind of warm inside, and he must remember to tip her. It was as if his body felt cared for... almost... he felt connected to her, like he could share...

Bodies thought they were whole, but pain lived in their spaces. For something that feared nothingness she did love the small jumps. Yet now chasms opened up. With each leap she was less, thinning out—dying. She would have to do... to do... that was it... what she had done when the last host died.

This was a good massage. Eleanor could feel the connection with the body.

But I will surely die. I cannot do it...

Simon took a long, full breath in, then out. Was it possible? Somewhere a distant part of him acknowledged he couldn't feel any pain, where had the pain gone? But he didn't want to be anywhere in particular at the moment, just in this relaxing nowhere space.

There is no story in the gap between thoughts. *And so space exists and the story ceases.*

Pain had no choice now. She leapt.

Time passed.

Nothing existed in something.

And then?

"Thank you, that was excellent," Simon said, raising his head cautiously from the cushioned headrest and taking in the therapist's silhouette against the bright window light.

"My pleasure," Eleanor said and waited patiently, her foot on the chair leg to stop slippage as he levered himself up off the chair and dismounted. He fumbled for his coat and wallet, pulling clear two crushed notes equalling £25, and a coin.

"Keep the change."

A pound. Well. Eleanor watched the man disconnect from her, come fully into himself and effortlessly straighten up, all smoothed out. Whole. She held the door open for him, and he turned briefly to look at her with a half-smile, as if already trying to place her in his mind. Then he was gone. She rolled her shoulders as she walked to the sink to wash her hands. She'd had four half hour massages earlier, yet it was that last forty-five minute massage that seemed to have wiped her out.

For a while it was as if Pain did not exist. Then as she came into herself she felt the difference. No longer thick and deep and nested, she was a stretched thing, light and transparent. It did not matter, she lived, clinging to the slippery surface of a thumb joint.

Eleanor ran the cold water tap and held her hands and lower arms in the water, then reached for the soap.

And Pain felt herself slip, down, down until she dangled from a fingertip.

She watched the water splash and dance across her skin, twisting her hands this way and that to relieve her aching thumb joints, then turned off the tap.

She hung on, only the warmth of inflammation providing traction, as she moved from cell to cell, and reached for the nerves.

Eleanor knew she'd over done it. She'd been working way too hard lately. Too many clients. You wanted to be helpful, but sometimes it was overwhelming. She just wasn't enough.

Oh how interesting. There were many shadows in this body. The shadows of others' pains.

She'd stop at the supermarket, maybe get a DVD. There was no rush getting back, not since, not since—

She would be different now, but yes, she could see this could be a good host. She ran quickly, stopping at all the small joints and the opportunities they offered.

She wiped her hands on the towel and her mind went there. Ever since he'd said it was all over. Ever since he'd—

There.

She flexed, and felt a jab of pain in her neck.

Oh yes, yes. Pain slid up and coiled around the neck. Here? Would this make a good nesting site? She hesitated then flickered up to the brain and back.

She rubbed her neck, just there. He would sit on the sofa and slip his hand to the back of her neck, his thumb caressing her jawline, there, where pleasure had once resided. She pulled on her coat and headed for the door. Puppet body, that's what she was, jerked by the strings of pain and pleasure. She'd get a bottle too, of red perhaps, she needed it.

Yes, good.

Try and forget that pain in her chest.

She could feel it now, the shadow map of the body. Her routes in. Pain found a place where the outbreath was unequal to the breath in. A balance pointing between inside and out, where she felt the undulation of the oesophagus unable to swallow the bolus of undigested sorrow.

She sank in and nested.

ESCAPING THE CITY

There is a thwump sound of something soft that travels under the car. This was real.

"What was that?" My daughter asks, but I already know. Looking into the car's rear mirror I see, or perhaps imagine, the fox raise its head a little before flopping back down onto the motorway tarmac.

She turns back and sees.

There is a silence so full, any parent knows what is to follow. It is the sound of a child's body blow shock, when they fall, or are hit, it is the pause as they suck in the air required.

Then wail.

Her primal keen blends with the awful pain in my chest. God, I am a killer.

"You killed him." She says. It's confirmed, I am a Murderer. The fox's head, that little lift, now plays like a screen shot, over and over behind my eyes. I change from the middle lane, to the slow lane, but there is nowhere to stop. Already, we are a quarter mile from the crime scene. But her howl is so loud it's painful in the tiny interior of the Citroen, and the vision so awful, I need to stop. I cannot pretend this hasn't happened.

"Is Foxy dead. Foxy is he dead." She demands wetly. The blame for this lies with me and her diet of fox myths. 'The Fox and the Red Hen', 'Fantastic Mr Fox', even the cartoon version of Robin Hood, is played by a Fox. Therefore 'Foxy' is not a real animal that tumbles under mum's car wheels, but a stuffed toy, a fable, an immortal story.

I am frantic for a layby, but the motorway ignores the surrounding countryside, simply pushes straight through, linking city to city. I am not meant to stop. No interaction between the black tarmac'd line delineated with crash barriers, and the anodyne countryside is expected or wished for. Travelling at 50 mph, I am encapsulated, trapped by my daughter's raw grief, and my silent agony, for a full five minutes, before the motorway offers up a layby.

The car is barely stationary, before she snatches at the handle and is out. Her door swings open, its arc stopped as the bottom of the door digs into a muddicd mound of blackened grass. I follow her, but there is a look in her eye, like she is too raw to hug. So I come round to her side, my heels sinking into the mud, but her expression is so full of wrath I have to look away. Is it this fox, or is it more? I am the focus of all her rage and my guilt snowballs, blurs with other larger and older culpabilities. Because what parent hasn't dragged their debris through their child's life. Stupid self-pitying tears threaten to fall, so I take a few muddied steps into the begrimed undergrowth, but the bank rises sharply.

There is no waiting welcome for this city foreigner into the countryside. I cross my arms as the cold wind snaps at my short sleeves. A row of black birds, sway on the branch of a scratchy bare tree, and examine the scene. Eye's bright. Yellow beaks move. They are passing judgement, but the thunder of the motorway drowns out the verdict. Where the countryside abuts the motorway, they are denied their voice.

I look back at her, ready to time my approach. Then see it - behind her.

More roadkill.

A trail of chestnut feathers, like footsteps, lead to its body, entrails bright and mashed flat, with its tail still tufted upright. No mercy shown. Any minute now, she will turn and see more death, so I jerk forwards and take her in an embrace. Is it a hug, or a restraint? Her body feels hard and she gives me nothing. She only calms down when I whisper to her, that he was only stunned and I saw him get up and trot away. That's right, I say, that cunning fox had us fooled. All the while that little lift and slump of the fox's head plays out in my head. I can say this, because he is not real. Lying on her pink pillow, Foxy is joined by Badger, and Squirrelly and Bear with his stitched smile.

I coax her back into our warm car bubble, under the stern gaze of the jury of black birds behind me. Us urban interlopers are not wanted in this wasteland that bears no resemblance to 'Escape to the Country', or 'Naturewatch'.

I grip the wheel tight and stare unblinking, with my right foot ready for the brake pedal, as five slow miles unfold. Grateful that she stares only at the Nintendo in her lap, whilst I mentally count the corpses of; two foxes, one rabbit, a hedgehog, and what I think could have been a squirrel. The countryside is a place inhabited by dead things, I think as I oh so carefully drive the way I came, back to the city.

As the motorway holds me and guides me, I think about my house. I promise myself I'll make a home of it. That I'll change my story, for my daughter's sake. The clearly delineated lines of the motorway flash by rhythmically and I allow myself to be soothed. I can do it, I will vow to play by the rules from now on. No more roaming the streets at all hours. No more make believe. No more playing the outsider. And contained in my car I believe I can cut

154

that memory clean out, just like I can detach myself from the green hell called the countryside. After a few miles all I see is exactly what is in front of me; a series of roundabouts, flanked by large concrete depots and warehouses. We are entering our city, and I am wrapped back in familiar urban grey.

And I tell myself that there are thousands and thousands of foxes, and that it wasn't her. It couldn't be my fox.

But that night I throw the window open and listen out for her. I lie awake in insomniac hell and wait, because I want my vixen back.

The answering silence is dark and huge, an emptiness that echoes beyond the core of me.

Tales of Urban Encounters is available in e-book and audiobook form.

If you have enjoyed these stories, receive a FREE short story by joining the mailing list at www.gerrymarsh.co.uk.

#writergerry

Made in the USA
Lexington, KY
02 July 2018